"Why didn't you ___
and le___

Rupert ___ ___ ___s
a perfe___ ___
what yo___

Sarah loo___ ___ him with distaste. "I
would have said basic, rather than
simple."

"By God, I'll make you listen
somehow!" Still holding her with one
hand, Rupert began to search in the
breast pocket of his waistcoat. He
produced a turquoise and diamond
ring and drew the thin doeskin glove
from her left hand. But at the sight of
five great sapphires glittering on her
ring finger, he dropped her hand
abruptly and pushed the turquoise
ring back into his pocket with
unsteady fingers.

"I'll return you to the donor of that
rather flamboyant little trifle you're
sporting," he murmured. "It seems
explanations are necessary on
both sides."

Books by Catherine George

HARLEQUIN PRESENTS

640—GILDED CAGE
698—IMPERFECT CHAPERONE
722—DEVIL WITHIN
800—PRODIGAL SISTER

HARLEQUIN ROMANCE

2535—RELUCTANT PARAGON
2571—DREAM OF MIDSUMMER

These books may be available at your local bookseller.

Don't miss any of our special offers. Write to us at the following address for information on our newest releases.

Harlequin Reader Service
P.O. Box 52040, Phoenix, AZ 85072-2040
Canadian address: P.O. Box 2800, Postal Station A,
5170 Yonge St., Willowdale, Ont. M2N 6J3

CATHERINE GEORGE

prodigal sister

Harlequin Books

TORONTO • NEW YORK • LONDON
AMSTERDAM • PARIS • SYDNEY • HAMBURG
STOCKHOLM • ATHENS • TOKYO • MILAN

Harlequin Presents first edition July 1985
ISBN 0-373-10800-1

Original hardcover edition published in 1984
by Mills & Boon Limited

CHAPTER ONE

THE girl sat perfectly still in her corner seat, her hands folded in her lap, gazing through the train window as though some picturesque sylvan landscape lay on the other side instead of the murk of Paddington Station. Intrigued, the man opposite turned his head to see what held her in thrall, but apart from a few porters' trolleys and the train standing at the next platform there seemed nothing to warrant such complete absorption.

She was worth looking at. From behind his newspaper her fellow-traveller studied her face covertly, wishing that more of it was visible. Her hair was glossy, raven-black, and cut in a short, expensively careless style to lie across her forehead, almost meeting the white-framed lenses of her sunglasses. Her nose tilted slightly above a rather wide, full mouth, and square decisive jaw, and however much he told himself he was imagining things, in some indefinable way she was familiar. He could swear he knew her. Frowning, he turned to the day's news, but her face came between his eyes and the printed page. Perhaps she was on television. He looked up quickly as the train gave a jerk and began to slide along the platform, but the sudden movement brought no reaction from the girl. As they left the gloom of the station her eyes remain fixed, unseeing, as the train emerged into sunshine and the stifling atmosphere of London in the grip of a sweltering July heatwave.

The lady looked cool, apparently unaffected by the hot yellow light slanting through the window. Her black silk blouse was dotted in white, and a white jacket of some kind lay folded neatly on the seat beside her. Both looked expensive. No rings were visible on her loosely clasped fingers, but at this point he checked his thoughts irritably and applied himself to the cricket scores. Even so he

5

found himself speculating on how far she was travelling, hoping it was somewhere more distant than Slough or Swindon, though from her present state of abstraction it seemed more than likely she might pass her destination without realising it.

Unaware of her fellow traveller, or his interest, Sarah Morgan sat in misery. Blind to her surroundings her eyes were turned inwards, seeing only the morning's events that had sent her running headlong out of the house in St John's Wood to make her way to Paddington by taxi, burdened by a large suitcase and the silly striped hatbox that now sat on the rack above her head. Her blank eyes could see only one scene, repeating itself endlessly in her mind; a video tape that went on and on ad nauseam. A vague, barely recognised instinct prompted her to give in to her grief and weep her disillusion away, but she ignored it, sitting upright and still, impaled like a butterfly on the pin of her mental peep-show.

The ticket-inspector finally broke through her reverie with his request, and Sarah came to with a start, searching in her handbag for the necessary ticket and handing it over to be clipped. As she put it back she saw there was a man sitting opposite her, partly hidden by his newspaper. Her eyes slid past him without interest as she resumed her former position, grateful to the ticket-inspector for interrupting her abstraction as she watched the dry, sun-drenched fields flashing by. Idly she glanced at the man opposite, but he was deeply intent on the sports page of his newspaper, apparently unaware that her eyes focused suddenly on his face. Like herself he wore dark glasses, but with dismay Sarah recognised him at once. This was definitely not her day. It was years since she'd seen him, but the man was unmistakable just the same. Hardly surprising since both of them had been born and brought up in the same part of the world, near Monmouth—Sarah Morgan, the Rector's daughter, and Rhodri Lloyd-Ellis, son and heir of Cwmderwen Court. He was looking in her direction now, a half-smile on his attractive face.

Sarah turned away, deliberately resuming her study of the passing landscape. She knew very well he was speculating about her identity. It gave her a feeling of superiority to sit with face averted, well aware he was searching for some excuse to strike up a conversation. The opportunity came sooner than expected, frightening the life out of her. As the train gathered speed, clattering over points in the track, the hatbox leapt off the rack, giving her head a glancing blow before coming to rest in Rhodri Lloyd-Ellis's outstretched hands. He sprang to his feet, leaning across the table in concern as Sarah's cheeks paled and she blinked, putting a hand to her head.

'I say, are you all right?' His voice was anxious. 'Did it hurt you?'

Sarah smiled, embarrassed. 'No. I'm fine, really. Startled a little, that's all.'

'Hang on a moment.'

He went through the connecting door, leaving her alone, and Sarah sat breathing deeply, looking at the gaily striped box with dislike. Her mother had insisted she buy a hat for the wedding, a quite unnecessary expense in Sarah's opinion, and now the wretched thing had made it necessary to indulge in polite conversation for the rest of the journey, unless she was mistaken. She looked up with a cool little smile as her involuntary knight-errant returned with a styrofoam beaker of hot coffee. She took it with a word of thanks, the colour rising in her cheeks after the first mouthful.

'I put a tot of brandy in it,' he said with a grin. 'You looked as though you needed it.'

'Thank you,' said Sarah. She eyed the coffee warily. 'I'll treat it with respect—I'm not really a brandy drinker.' She removed the sunglasses as the lenses steamed up from the heat of the drink and looked up at her companion. 'Please let me pay you for the drink.'

He shook his head. 'Please. It was the least I could do.'

Her eyebrows rose.

'Why? Did you knock the box off the rack?'

He smiled, showing even white teeth in a smile Sarah

remembered very well from the days when he occasionally came to the Rectory with her brother, Gareth.

'No. But I was trying to think of some way to get into conversation with you. All that occurred to me was the old chestnut "haven't I seen you somewhere before?"— hardly the most inspired of openers, you must admit. Nevertheless, I do have this strong feeling I know you. Are you on television, or something?'

Sarah finished her coffee. The brandy in it had relaxed her considerably, and she looked into the handsome face of her inquisitor with a faint, enigmatic smile.

'I'm not on television, but you do know me slightly. At least you did, a few years ago.'

He scanned her face, frowning.

'If I knew you a few years ago you must have been very young.'

'Not necessarily.' Sarah smiled at him indulgently. 'Women have all sorts of tricks to stave off age, you know.'

'You're enjoying this.' Rhodri smiled, shrugging. 'All right. We'll play it your way. Twenty questions. You must come from my part of the world—no disguising that certain cadence in the voice.'

Sarah inclined her head.

'From Monmouth?' he went on. 'No? Cwmderwen itself then?'

'Right.'

His eyes narrowed.

'Not exactly a teeming metropolis—I ought to know at once.' His eyes widened suddenly. 'Are you a relative of the Morgans?'

'Which Morgans?'

'The Rector's family.'

'Yes.'

'A cousin?'

'No.'

'Am I getting warmer?'

Suddenly Sarah tired of the game.

'Look at me carefully,' she said.

'I haven't been able to *stop* looking since I got on the train, but I'm still none the wiser.' He frowned in concentration.

'I used to look a bit different. For starters I was over a stone heavier. Now I have a dent in my nose, my jaw's more pronounced and my eyes are different, sort of elongated instead of round.' She stopped as Rhodri nodded slowly.

'Not Rhia . . . no, of course! Sarah; you were in a car accident with Rhia!'

Sarah nodded matter-of-factly. 'My face was a bit knocked about.'

'Rhia was all right though, wasn't she?'

'The sun always shines on the righteous—isn't that the way it goes?' Sarah was purposely flippant. 'Let's hope it shines tomorrow—that's my wedding hat.'

Rhodri's head came up sharply. 'You're getting married tomorrow?'

She gave him the full benefit of the lopsided smile that was another of her legacies from the accident.

'No. Rhia is the blushing bride.'

To her surprise he seemed relieved, his eyes still intent on her face.

'You had no difficulty in remembering me then, Sarah?'

'Of course not, despite the film-star shades. Rhodri Lloyd-Ellis, the local squire, or at least you will be one day. How could I forget? Your hair is a shade darker now, of course. Besides I had a terrible crush on you when I was sixteen, but I was at the roly-poly stage and you had eyes only for Rhia—in common with all the male populace within a ten-mile radius.'

'Do I detect a sibling jealousy?' asked Rhodri lightly.

'No. At least not any more.' Sarah glanced away through the window. 'At one time I resented her a bit, envied her looks, but I grew out of that.'

Rhodri sat watching her averted face for a time.

'How are you getting home from Newport, Sarah?' he asked eventually.

She turned the distinctive Morgan eyes on him, bright turquoise blue, startling beneath her black brows.

'I hadn't really thought that far yet. A bus, I suppose, or I expect someone will come and fetch me if I ring home. I did try at Paddington before the train left, but there was no answer. Probably they were at the hairdressers, or doing the flowers or something.'

'Aren't you expected on this train?' He was curious. Her travel plans sounded rather vague.

A shadow darkened Sarah's face.

'I was supposed to be driving down—with a friend. He was coming to the wedding. I was even childish enough to keep his identity a secret from the family.' Self-derision flickered in her mocking smile. 'I was so smug about the surprise everyone would have when I turned up with my new fiancé. Childish, wasn't it?'

'What happened?' he asked quietly, his face sympathetic.

Sarah traced a pattern on the table with an idle fingernail.

'The engagement terminated—abruptly—this morning. So I made a run for Paddington, boarded this train, and here we are.' She laughed. 'The only reason I'm travelling first class is because I wasn't paying enough attention when I bought my ticket. Do you travel often by train?'

Rhodri Lloyd-Ellis was deeply curious about the background to Sarah's little story, but it was plain she already regretted having said so much.

'Hardly ever,' he answered, and took off his dark glasses with a flourish. 'But I didn't feel like driving west along the M4 into the sun with this.'

'Wow!' said Sarah in awe. 'What's the other chap like?'

Rhodri had attractive, humorous eyes, grey, with very clear whites and laughter-lines at the corners, but at the moment one of them was partly closed and surrounded by a contusion in delicate shades of plum and navy-blue. He put the glasses on again and leaned across the table, smiling.

'I beat him into the dust—well, squash court to be accurate. I managed to get in the way of the ball right at the end, unfortunately.'

Sarah looked at the breadth of his shoulders in the stud-fastened cream linen shirt.

'You keep pretty fit for a banker, or stockbroker, or whatever it is that you do. "Something in the city" I think I heard somewhere.'

Rhodri settled back in his seat. 'Something like that. I'm with a merchant bank pro tem, but in my spare time I play quite a bit of squash and frequent the gym at my club as often as possible. I try to get down to Cwnderwen regularly too, and give a hand on the farm when I'm there—keeping my finger on the agricultural pulse of my heritage, as it were. My mother's getting old, and I shall have to take over the reins entirely soon.'

'How *is* Lady Marian?'

'Getting more and more fragile physically. Otherwise she's as indomitable as ever——' He broke off. 'Was your mother expecting you at any particular time?'

Sarah's eyes dropped.

'No. I said we'd arrive some time tonight—after dinner. I had intended to work all this morning, then we were driving to Monmouth, where my—my erstwhile chum was booked in for the weekend. The plan was to arrive at the Rectory about nine and spare Mother two dinner guests, at least.' She smiled crookedly. 'One of those best-laid plans obviously.'

'Then may I offer you a lift?'

'How are you going to manage that?' asked Sarah curiously.

'Dic Richards, our farm manager, will have left my car at the station. I have a spare set of keys.' He looked at her enquiringly.

Sarah looked back for a moment, then accepted. 'Thank you very much. How kind of you—practically a one-man rescue operation.' She gave him a funny little grin. 'I hope you know what you're taking on.'

He looked puzzled. 'I don't follow.'

Sarah shrugged and spread her hands. 'You must be aware that I'm the black sheep of the family. Memories are long in Cwmderwen; to the village I'm still the Morgan girl who drove into a tree before passing her test.'

'Oh that! Isn't it time to put all that behind you?' he asked mildly.

'Yes, of course it is,' said Sarah quickly, then glanced out of the window as the train began to reduce speed. 'We're just coming in to Newport.' She stood up, putting an end to the conversation as Rhodri sprang to his feet to help her with her case.

Rhodri led the way to the station car park where he stowed their luggage in the boot of a brand new scarlet Porsche.

'What a beauty!' Sarah said in admiration.

'Nice isn't she?' he said casually. 'I left it here last weekend—now, Miss Morgan, as no one is expecting you at home, why not come and have some tea, or are you in a hurry?'

'Not in the least. Thank you, I'd love some tea.' The idea was welcome, to Sarah's surprise, as she suddenly realised that part of her hollow feeling was due to sheer hunger.

A short time later they were installed in a small, cosy tea-shop sharing a pot of tea and a large plateful of newly baked scones. Sarah licked her fingers inelegantly before refilling their tea cups.

'I enjoyed that,' she said with a sigh. 'I had no breakfast and missed lunch.'

'You should have had something more substantial. Have some more scones at least.' Rhodri signalled to the pretty young waitress, who hurried to refill the plate, casting forthright looks of admiration at Rhodri as she set the scones in front of him.

'She thinks you're a celebrity hiding behind those glasses,' observed Sarah with a grin. 'Look—she's positively scarlet with excitement.'

'Shall I take them off and disillusion her?'

'I doubt if it would. There's a certain machismo about a black eye.'

Rhodri looked taken aback. He stared at Sarah.

'Are you serious?'

She nodded solemnly. 'Though to be fair I suppose only when someone's tall and rather beautiful like you, Rhodri.'

He sat back in his chair and removed the glasses deliberately, his eyes narrowed as they scrutinised her face. 'Fighting talk, Sarah!'

'Take no notice, please,' she begged hastily. 'I'm really not myself today, one way and another.'

Rhodri put out a hand and touched hers gently, his good-looking face warm with sympathy. 'Tell me about it.'

He felt a tremor run through her as she took her hand away and pushed it restlessly through the thick black hair falling over her forehead. She shook her head doubtfully.

'It's not really worth talking about—not even very interesting.'

The little waitress watched with a sigh as Rhodri leaned nearer to Sarah and took her hand firmly in his, looking very steadily into her unhappy blue eyes.

'It's not prurient curiosity, Sarah, but wouldn't you feel better if you got it off your chest to someone impartial? It's always easier to confide in strangers apparently. I'm not a stranger precisely, but at least we don't encounter each other often enough for you to be embarrassed because I know your guilty secret.' Rhodri's grasp tightened and he smiled reassuringly. 'Go on. Tell me what's wrong. What happened?'

'Where do you want me to start?' Sarah's eyes were quizzical.

He released her hand and leaned back in his seat comfortably, giving her a nod of encouragement. 'Fill me in on your life after the accident.'

Sarah looked at him, startled, biting her lip in indecision. The laughing grey eyes and thick curling fair hair of the man beside her had once haunted her youthful dreams, but his role had always been Prince Charming, not father-confessor. Bleakly she realised that she would have to keep her troubles to herself at home, with the entire family taken up with Rhia's wedding, and suddenly the overpowering need to talk to someone conquered her habitual reticence.

'For your ears only, then,' she said at last, deliberately flippant. 'I can see you're sitting comfortably, so I'll begin.'

CHAPTER TWO

AT eighteen Sarah Morgan's life took a sudden violent swerve in a different direction. When she was extricated from the wreck of her father's car to the sound of her sister's screams she was aware only of pain and fear until in the ambulance the blessed prick in her arm brought escape into limbo. Her physical injuries were mostly to her face, apart from a wrenched knee and a broken bone in her foot, but bit by bit she recovered from them all with youthful resilience, a double fracture of her jaw, a broken nose, black eyes, various cuts and lacerations and a couple of shattered back teeth. She had, they said, been lucky. She had made contact with the windscreen without actually going through it. Sarah was deeply grateful to the surgeon who restored her face to normality. There were no lasting scars but her face was unavoidably a little different. Nothing could alter the blue of her eyes, but plastic surgery on her scarred temples and cheeks had changed their shape from round to almond, and her nose had a definite dent at its bridge. Her cheekbones were more prominent than before, her mouth a little crooked, and the broken jaw never quite managed to resume its former place, but set square and uncompromising, adding a look of decision to her face entirely lacking prior to the accident.

Eight weeks of drinking fluids through the metal cast clamping her jaws together reduced Sarah's weight drastically. The roly-poly teenager disappeared forever, replaced by a slim, withdrawn young woman who found life difficult once she was at home again. Her parents were loving and supportive, but Sarah was haunted by the knowledge that her father suffered deep disillusion beneath the tenderness, unable to forget that Sarah had risked not only her own life but that of her sister's by driving illegally and too fast along a tortuous road at night.

Sarah's brother Gareth was a doctor, already married and living in Warwickshire, and apart from a flying visit when the accident first happened she saw little of him to her relief, as, fond of him though she was, his bracing personality was inclined to be exhausting. Her sister Rhiannon escaped from the accident without a mark on the beautiful face that was already beginning to earn her a considerable amount in London as a top model. She haunted her sister's bedside for the first few days, engaging her in low-toned, pleading conversation whenever she was left alone with the patient for a few minutes. Rhia's deep anxiety for her sister was much lauded by the nursing staff, who privately considered Rhia had every right to blame Sarah for endangering both their lives in such an irresponsible manner. Eventually Rhia had to leave for a modelling assignment in the Bahamas, and not long afterwards Sarah was allowed home. Back in the rectory it was the baby of the family, fourteen-year-old Mari-Sîan, who was Sarah's greatest comfort, teasing her about her scars, calling her 'Jaws' and generally treating her like a normal person. Try as she might to be casual Mrs Morgan coddled her injured child too much, showering her with love to demonstrate that Sarah's foolishness had made no difference to her mother's affections. All too often Sarah felt smothered, then racked with guilt at her own ingratitude. Yet for some reason her father's forbearance was even harder to endure, and Sarah spent many a long sleepless night wishing he knew the real reason why she had been at the wheel of the wrecked car. Since she herself had been the one determined to say nothing, insisting that she remembered nothing at all and making Rhia promise to bear her out, it was too late afterwards to change her mind.

The accident put an end to Sarah's plans to read history at the University of York. Her place would have been kept for her until the following year, and at first

Sarah fully intended to take it up, spending the intervening year quietly at home getting fit again, her convalescence hastened by the departure of the nightmares that had plagued her during the first weeks after the accident. Very soon it became obvious that she could never stick it out. Sarah was too young and too vulnerable not to care deeply when she found some people were no longer quite so friendly. At the village shops she was conscious of hastily averted eyes and a tinge of awkwardness, and even coolness where previously she had only experienced warmth. Even this was preferable to the open curiosity of the less sensitive, who stared frankly at her remodelled face and her newly healed scars, and even probed for details of the crash. Attendance at church became purgatory as, imagined or otherwise, Sarah felt all eyes were turned in her direction.

Sarah grew reserved and introspective, holding out only as long as it took to feel strong again, then shocked her parents by rejecting her university place and announcing she was off to a secretarial college in London. She hungered for solitude and independence, and finally, reluctantly, Glyn and Elizabeth Morgan let her go with their anxious blessing.

After the insular quiet of a small village the sheer noise and pace of life in London was at once alarming and therapeutic. Sarah was intimidated at first, yet at the same time fervently glad of her welcome anonymity in the crowd. In Cwmderwen she was the Rector's daughter, hardly able to set foot outside the door without meeting someone who knew about the accident. In London not a soul knew or cared, and this in itself was balm to Sarah's spirit, more than compensating for periods of searing loneliness in her hostel room.

Sarah put her ambitions to teach history behind her and threw herself into her new studies with a will, quickly becoming proficient at typing, and eventually able to take shorthand at speed in both English and French. She made friends with other girls on the course and went out with groups of them at night, and little by little her inner anguish began to subside. She went home at intervals for short visits, but never went to church and kept away from the village, restricting herself to the confines of the Rectory, or to Monmouth.

On completion of her course the post-finder bureau of the secretarial college placed Sarah with a well-known agency for temps, and two of the other girls there soon asked her to share their flat. The quality of Sarah's life improved. Through her flatmates, Alison and Dinah, Sarah met numbers of young men, which livened up her evenings enormously, though Sarah preferred to go out in a crowd, not caring for invitations from any one man in particular, to the amusement of her friends. As part of a noisy, cheerful group Sarah had no qualms, but on a one to one basis people were inclined to ask for personal details which Sarah had no wish to provide.

Sarah liked the variety and irregularity of her job, enjoying a week here and a month there, gaining useful experience in various branches of commerce in the process, until the day the agency received an anguished call from Rupert Clare. One-time journalist, now the super-successful author of several best-selling historical novels, with film and television rights under his belt, his books automatically hit the top of the popularity lists as soon as they were published. His demand was for someone who could spell and write good English, had a fairly conservative appearance, an effacing personality and a reasonable education behind her. Miss Frobisher, who ran the agency on oiled wheels, assured him in glacial tones that *all* her young ladies fitted his description. However, in view of Sarah's leanings towards history, she was the one chosen to go along to the elegant Georgian house in St John's Wood.

Rupert Clare's long-standing association with beautiful young actress Naomi Prentiss was in the process of dissolution at roughly the same time a stomach bug struck down his secretary, half-way through the book he was writing. When Mrs Dobson, his placid and stoic housekeeper, led a tense Sarah across the imposing hall to a study overlooking the secluded, walled garden at the back of the house, Rupert Clare was standing at the window, staring moodily into space. Sarah had devoured every word ever written by him, and was familiar with his face from the dust jackets of his novels. Nevertheless, when he swung round to look at her for the first time she was utterly unprepared for the impact of the look that swept her up and down in frank appraisal beneath the shock of thick brown hair hanging untidily over his forehead. His eyes were an opaque dark green, like bottleglass, beneath brows even thicker and more uncompromising than her own. Sarah took one look and was lost. She fell fathoms deep in love quite literally at first sight. To her everlasting gratitude the iron control so dearly bought kept her face blank and expressionless as she gazed silently at the man who seemed the embodiment of her every dream. He returned her unblinking stare, nodding slowly, one long finger rubbing his blunt, straight nose.

'You know what I expect?' he asked.

'Not precisely.' Sarah met the dissecting stare with composure, inwardly amazed when her voice functioned quite normally.

'The job means irregular hours, hard work, and an aptitude for research. It requires a calm temperament to complement mine, which is filthy, and furthermore I have no idea how long you'll be needed. It might be a week, or even a month if my secretary has an appendix or something instead of a stomach bug.'

In actual fact the secretary's 'or something' proved to be pregnancy, and she never returned to work for Rupert Clare again, apparently unable to cope with both the job and early morning sickness. So Sarah became a permanent secretary cum researcher. She took to the work like a duck to water, starting each day by typing the cassettes Rupert dictated the day, or night, before. He worked when and where the fancy took him, often far into the night if the flow was flowing, and if the spate slowed Sarah sometimes provided the inspiration to re-start it. In addition to this the meticulous research he demanded was sheer delight to her, and the only fly in the ointment was Rupert's temperament. For the first six months Sarah worked for him Rupert was openly moody and irritable, still smarting from the break-up with the beautiful and talented Naomi, whose career on the stage progressed by leaps and bounds, with a good deal of attendant publicity. Sarah resolutely banked down the smouldering fire of her own secret feelings and trod warily, learning to gauge Rupert's mood almost as soon as she let herself into the house each morning with the key he gave her.

As he grew to know Sarah better he liked to talk to her, confide in her even on times. 'It isn't as if Naomi left me for another man,' he said to her once, even more morose than usual. 'Her whole life was geared towards her career, and the same thing applied to me. Combination of the two just wouldn't work and her career was more important to her than I was, so off she went. We still remain friends—but I miss her.'

Secretly cut to ribbons by his last words Sarah maintained a sympathetic front, impersonal and efficient at the same time. Rupert gave her a rise in wages to compensate for his gloom and misery. The extra money coincided with Dinah's wedding and Alison's emigration to Australia, so Sarah found a smaller flat only a short journey away on the underground, and occupied it alone, which she found she now preferred. She had her hair cut expertly into a short, forehead-swathing style, joined a health club to keep her figure in trim, and invested in some rather more adventurous clothes. Her heart remained dented, but otherwise her self-confidence and poise received a definite boost. This was fortunate, as Rupert was about to embark on what she privately called his 'rehabilitation phase', which included wining and dining as many beautiful, glamorous women as was physically possible, 'physical' being the operative word. Secretly eaten up with jealousy Sarah went on researching and typing his drafts, but now found herself lumbered with the additional, and highly unwelcome, chore of juggling Rupert's social engagements, not to mention coping with the stream of nubile femininity that beat a path to his lovingly restored front door.

Rupert Clare's bad-tempered good looks and tall, graceful body would have been enough—more than enough in Sarah's opinion—but allied to his income, plus the sweet smell of success that was his perpetual aura, he was downright irresistible to all the women he met. Sarah had been working for him for more than two years before it finally dawned on him that his secretary was not at one on this point with the rest of her sex. She was friendly, efficient, even-tempered and very, very wary of this new phase that Rupert showed alarming signs of entering. She met subtle overtures of friendship with good-humoured, polite nonchalance, adroitly avoiding him whenever possible, determined to keep their relationship on a strictly employer/secretary footing. Sarah liked her job, and despite an inward, urgent desire to respond to him, saw all too clearly what happened to those foolish enough to become besotted with Rupert Clare. To her fell the unwelcome task of making excuses on the phone, giving tactful, if untruthful, explanations for his absence, and even mopping up tears when the less timid arrived in person, demanding to see Rupert, only to find he flatly refused to emerge from the enormous room upstairs which gave him the necessary space to stalk up and down like an erudite panther while dictating, as well as for the king-sized bed with the Hockney on the recessed wall behind it.

At first Rupert was nettled by Sarah's apparent indifference to his wakening interest in her, then intrigued, then finally in open pursuit. His role switched from quarry to hunter, and he grew remorseless in his goal of getting Sarah where he wanted her, presumably in his king-sized bed. She was not altogether sure about this as, to do him justice, since Naomi's departure he had never brought any of his casual conquests home to share the aforesaid bed, a fact confirmed by Mrs Dobson, the housekeeper. Presumably when they said 'your place or mine?' he always said 'yours'. But Sarah remembered the succession of newspaper pictures of Rupert with blonde at Annabel's, Rupert with redhead at first night, and so on, also the long weekends in Paris and Rome on so-called research, and went on resolutely fending Rupert off. She continued to go out now and then with the young trainee accountant who lived in the flat below hers, and had an occasional date with the judo instructor at her health club, and never for an instant gave Rupert an inkling of how increasingly difficult she found it to fake indifference to the devastating battery of his charm, now apparently trained solely on herself. There were less and less phone calls from demanding females, no longer was the front door assaulted by glossy young women clamouring for entrance, and the tabloids were devoid of shots of Rupert smouldering away into the bemused eyes of some poor, dazzled female.

Work on the latest novel was reaching its climax. For days Rupert was shut away in his room dictating incessantly, until, finally, one afternoon he staggered into the study where Sarah was typing furiously, threw a pile of cassettes on the rosewood table that served as her desk and flung himself down on the velvet-covered chaise longue near the window, one arm dramatically across his eyes.

'I've finished,' he announced.

Sarah went on typing, unconcerned.

Rupert sprang to his feet and switched off the cassette recorder.

'I said I've finished, Sarah,' he roared.

Sarah removed her earphones and laid them on the table.

'Great,' she said shortly, and looked pointedly at the pile of cassettes still waiting to be typed. 'I haven't.'

Rupert thrust a hand through his hair and glared at her. 'Don't you ever get excited about anything?'

'Not if I can possibly help it.' She looked at him patiently. 'Can I get on now, please?'

He scowled at her. He was barefoot, dressed in a running-vest and the bottom half of a track suit, and needed a shave badly. There were dark marks like bruises under the celebrated eyes, he was in crying need of a haircut, and Sarah suddenly scented danger. He pounced, tore the lead of her typewriter from its socket, and hauled Sarah out of her chair and into his arms, kissing her with a ferocity and avidity that dazed and excited her to the point of becoming almost like putty in his embrace. But not quite.

'You're driving me mad, woman,' he groaned, and picked her up.

'Then one of us had better stay sane,' she retorted, breathless, but resolute. 'I flatly refuse to join the serried ranks of your playmates, so please put me down.'

There was a long, long pause while Rupert stood with Sarah in his arms, breathing hard, his eyes boring into hers, willing her into compliance.

'No?' he said softly.

Sarah swallowed hard and shook her head firmly, hoping the thudding in her chest was inaudible to him. 'No, Rupert.'

Instead of setting her on her feet Rupert sat down on the chaise longue, with Sarah on his lap. 'There's only one thing for it, then—we'd better get married,' he said, surprisingly gauche for one so well-versed in prose.

Sarah's eyes narrowed to a blue astonished glitter. 'Are you serious?'

'Yes. Perfectly serious.' There was a smug look of self-congratulation on his face as he looked down at her.

'If it's a bedfellow you're after there are plenty willing to accommodate you without resorting to anything as desperate as marriage,' she said tartly, trying, and failing, to breathe normally.

'But none with a brain and a disposition like yours, my Welsh dragon.' Rupert kissed her lightly and held her closer. 'Not to mention the package they come in—small, but very, very tempting.' This time the kiss was anything but light, and Sarah's response was involuntary as she yielded to the expert, practised hands and mouth, her defences wobbling perilously.

'What about the others?' she panted, pushing at him with trembling hands.

Rupert frowned down at her flushed face. 'What others?'

Sarah's jaw set in a way he had come to recognise. 'I can only count from Naomi Prentiss onwards, but even so your score of conquests is impressive by any standards. Would marriage to me automatically cancel out the rest, or would I always be wondering who you were with the moment my back was turned?'

Rupert shook her roughly, then grinned down at her with a wicked gleam dancing in his eyes. 'You're jealous!' he said in delight, and began to kiss her again until she was helpless and yielding in his arms. 'Look at me, Sarah,' he commanded at long last.

Sarah's heavy lids rose and she gazed up at him, her breath catching as she saw the passionate sincerity in Rupert's, which glowed like tourmalines as they held hers.

'Never anyone but you, my darling, ever again,' he said huskily. 'I promise—see? Cross my heart and hope to die. It's God's truth, Sarah, so will you marry me?'

Sarah looked at him searchingly for several more moments, then she gave him a small, uncertain smile. 'Yes please, Rupert.'

With an exclamation of relief he caught her cruelly tight, kissing her exuberantly all over her face, his lips finally hovering a fraction away from hers. 'Move in with me until I get a special licence,' he muttered against her mouth, his face flushing darkly as he felt her melt against him.

Sarah stiffened and sat up, pushing his arms away with determination.

'No,' she said baldly.

'For God's sake, why not?' He grasped her forearms, his eyes blazing into hers. 'You practically live here now—what's the difference?'

'I don't *sleep* here, that's the difference.' She sighed. 'Besides, my father's a clergyman. He will naturally expect me to be married in the church at home.' She stood up and walked over to the window, her back to him. 'Don't worry, I won't hold you to it, you know. We can just forget this little episode and carry on as before.'

Rupert sprang up and followed her, his hands biting into her shoulders as he spun Sarah to face him. He was in deadly earnest as he said, 'We can cut our wrists and mingle the blood, or leap over a bonfire, or any way you choose, Sarah, but I meant every word. I want you to marry me, all right, and the sooner the better. I don't much mind where or how we tie the knot, as long as it's soon. My life of celibacy is something of a strain.'

Sarah looked searchingly into his eyes for some time, then nodded. 'Right. I'll ring my parents tonight.'

When Rupert finally let her go home much later that evening Sarah could hear the telephone ringing as she opened the door of her flat. It was her mother, with a piece of news Sarah received with mixed feelings. Rhia was getting married. Trust Rhia to get in first, thought Sarah. She was marrying Sir Charles Hadley, an industrialist, a widower with two little motherless girls from a first marriage, and the wedding would be in her father's church, of course, and she hoped Sarah would act as bridesmaid. Sarah's mouth went dry at the thought.

'Mother, don't be hurt, but I would so much rather not,' she said carefully. 'I know my face is all right now, but since it was done over people still stare at me in Cwmderwen as if I were some sort of freak. Weak spirited of me I know, but I find it hard to take. The thought of walking down the aisle as bridesmaid, let alone posing for photographs, brings me out in a rash. I'll come as a guest and mingle with the crowd with pleasure, but apologise to Rhia about the rest.'

'Yes, of course,' said her mother, obviously disappointed. 'Rhia will understand. Nevertheless she wanted you to know you'd been asked. You will be there, though?'

'Yes, I promise.'

'And you'll wear a hat?' There was a chuckle in her mother's voice. Sarah had always detested any form of headgear.

'Yes, I'll even wear a hat—but only to please you!'

Afterwards, when she was eating her supper, Sarah felt bitter as she realised her own news had never been announced.

'Why the hell not?' demanded Rupert next day.

'I preferred to leave it for a while.' Sarah eyed him warily. 'Now don't get aerated.'

'I'm not.' Rupert pulled her into his arms and stroked her head as it lay against his chest. 'I promise to contain my soul in patience.' Rupert raised her face to his with a wicked glint in his eyes. 'Only it's not exactly my soul that's giving me the trouble!' His mouth was on hers as he finished speaking and Sarah gave herself up to his lovemaking with rapture, deriving comfort as well as excitement as he held her close and murmured very gratifying things in her ear all the time his hands were moving over her in a way that brought her close to breaking point.

'Go away,' she said breathlessly at last, and gave him a push. 'Go jogging or something—I have work to do.'

Rupert moved to the door with the graceful swagger that caused such secret havoc inside Sarah. He swung round, frowning.

'What did you mean by "I"?' he demanded.

Sarah looked blank. 'I'm not with you.'

'You said "when *I* go to the wedding!" Let me come too; put up in the nearest town, and we could announce our own forthcoming union at the same time.'

His eyes darkened almost to black as Sarah's lit up like lamps and she ran across the room to fling her arms around his neck, pressing her face against his as she stood on tiptoe.

'I never imagined you'd want to come, Rupert.' She moved her head back and smiled at him, incandescent with gratitude. 'Thank you, darling.'

'My God,' he muttered unsteadily, and crushed her to him unmercifully. 'Smile at me much more like that and our "forthcoming union" is likely to have a date in advance of rather than after your sister's wedding! Go back to your typewriter, woman—I need a very cold shower.'

Sarah booked Rupert in at the King's Head in Monmouth for the weekend of Rhia's wedding, then set about finding something suitably ravishing to wear, refusing to let him pay for it, as he wished, even more adamant that she chose it alone.

'Your face is too well known,' she said firmly. 'You should have kept your social life out of the popular press. If you came with me I'd feel like a kept woman, as they used to call it.'

'I only wish you were,' he said hotly, and frustrated all her attempts to free herself, kissing her dizzy before allowing her to set out on her shopping spree.

Recklessly Sarah spent a good deal more than she had intended, closing her mind to the reasons. Praying the weather would be kind on the day, she eventually chose a slip-like knee-length dress in biscuit-coloured satin with its own hip-length jacket, and invested in a pair of satin shoes in the same shade. A natural straw boater with a black-edged white ribbon looked good set straight on her short, skilful haircut, and she found doeskin gloves and clutch-purse to round things off. Throwing caution to the winds she added a white-dotted black crêpe-de-chine blouse and slim black fly-fastened skirt to the costly little pile to wear with the white seersucker jacket she already possessed, after which she went back to St John's Wood to display her haul to Rupert, her bank-balance very much depleted.

'I blew all the money I've been saving for a holiday in Greece,' she told him ruefully.

'I could possibly scrape enough money for a honeymoon in the Greek Islands if that's what you'd like,' he said, his eyes gleaming.

Sarah flushed. 'I hadn't thought of that.'

'I envy you. Thoughts of our honeymoon occupy me to the exclusion of all else at the moment—even my next book.' He kissed her hard. 'Now show me this extravagant dress, then.'

The sky was a hazy blue, already bleached pale with heat when Sarah left her flat very early on the day before Rhia's wedding, weighed down with suitcase and frivolous striped hatbox. The journey on the Underground was enlivened by thoughts of stealing into the lovely house in St John's Wood long before Rupert was due to set out and collect her. She was eager to catch up on any typing that might have accumulated since the previous morning, slightly guilty about a whole afternoon at the hairdresser, followed by a quiet evening alone and an early night in preparation for today.

It was too early for Mrs Dobson, who did the marketing on her way in on Fridays, and the house was utterly still as Sarah let herself noiselessly in and tiptoed across the hall, leaving her suitcase and hatbox just inside the front door, with her white jacket neatly folded alongside. She made coffee in the kitchen, then took her cup into the semicircular conservatory at the back of the house and sat on one of the white-painted chairs to drink it, her eyes dreamy as she gazed out on the lawn while the sun rose higher, giving promise of the heat to come.

For once she decided to break her rule and take a cup of coffee up to Rupert's bedroom. Up to now she had never set foot across the threshold, but today was different. Today she would begin to wear the ring made specially for her to Rupert's instructions, diamonds and turquoises to match her eyes. She sighed happily and started up the curving stair with the coffee, tapped on his door and opened it without waiting for his reply. Sarah stood transfixed, staring in horror at the girl in the bed. It was Naomi Prentiss, her hair streaming over her bare shoulders, a look of humorous dismay on her beautiful face. Sarah recoiled as Rupert emerged from his bathroom, in a short, silk robe, his face stricken as he saw her in the doorway. The cup slid from Sarah's hand, the black liquid staining the carpet as she turned blindly away and careered down the curve of the stairs in headlong flight, gathering up her belongings in one fell swoop before opening the front door.

'Sarah, wait!' Rupert was half way down the stairs as she banged the door shut behind her and catapulted into Hamilton Terrace, running like one possessed, the suitcase banging against her legs as a taxi miraculously cruised to a halt beside her.

With a sob of relief Sarah threw her things into the taxi and told the driver to hurry.

'Where to, miss?'

'Anywhere,' she answered in anguish, 'just get me away from here.'

CHAPTER THREE

As Sarah finished her much-expurgated account of the story Rhodri Lloyd-Ellis pressed her hand in sympathy. 'There might have been a logical explanation, Sarah.'

She smiled with irony. 'Oh there was! If one finds a woman in Rupert Clare's bed there's always a perfectly logical explanation—the obvious one! I fail to see what other explanation there could possibly be. Without embarrassing you with the mawkish details perhaps I should explain that Rupert had been quite eloquent on the subject of needing only one woman for the rest of his life. Me.' A shudder of distaste ran through her. 'What really makes my skin crawl is that it was Naomi Prentiss in his bed, as though she were a habit he found impossible to break. All the others since were unimportant, but he really *cared* for her.'

Rhodri looked at Sarah's stormy face with compassion, obviously at a loss for words to comfort her, then turned to summon the hovering waitress for the bill.

The sun was still hot as they walked along the crowded High Street, thronged at this time of day with Friday shoppers. Sarah's feelings were mixed. In one way she felt admittedly better for pouring out her tale of woe to the man beside her. She had told only the bare bones of the story, admittedly, leaving out the emotions and the private, personal bits, but even so half of her felt an irrational disloyalty to Rupert, while the other half shrugged this off, experiencing relief at having had someone to talk to about it.

'Which particular factor of the incident is upsetting you most, Sarah?' Rhodri asked as they reached the car.

'One that's very superficial and petty, I'm ashamed to confess. Last night I yielded to childish temptation and told Mother my mystery guest was the man I intended to marry, and made it even worse by getting all coy and withholding his identity, with the idea of springing Rupert on them as a surprise. How stupid can one get!'

Rhodri made no comment as he handed her into the Porsche. Sarah watched his tall, athletic figure as he crossed to the driver's seat. He was muscular yet elegant in the fawn casual jacket and well-cut pleated trousers, with none of the swagger that was so characteristic of Rupert. Forget Rupert, she told herself savagely, blinking hard to stop the tears that sprang hot and unbidden to her eyes, glad of her concealing sunglasses. She tried to concentrate on the luxury of the car's interior, but all she could see was Naomi's flushed guilty face and the consternation in Rupert's green eyes. The great pity of it all, thought Sarah in misery, was that the blind instinct which had sent her racing from Rupert's house had failed to kill her love for him at the same time. Instead of which it seemed to rage inside her as strong as ever, not in the least diminished by her searing disillusion. She took a tissue from her bag and carefully blotted her eyes, hoping Rhodri wouldn't notice as he concentrated on the traffic. The main thing occupying her at the moment, taking precedence even over her unhappiness, was the thought of arriving home without her mysterious escort. How amused Rhia would be. Why did everything go on smoothly for the Rhias of this world, thought Sarah resentfully, when for herself things invariably went horribly wrong?

'Still feeling wretched, Sarah?' asked Rhodri quietly.

Sarah wrenched herself out of her cloud of self-pity, ashamed of her bad manners. 'I do apologise, Rhodri. I must try and snap out of it. You caught me at a bad time, I'm afraid.'

'The man's an idiot,' he said tersely, his eyes on the road.

'I'm the idiot,' she said bleakly, then gave an irritable little shake of her head. 'To be candid, what's bothering me most of all at this minute is having to turn up at home *sans* fiancé—which gives you some idea of how shallow and petty I can be at times.'

'Human is the word I'd use.'

Sarah turned a grateful smile on him. 'Thank you. You're sweet.' She turned away, frowning. 'What an evening it promises to be. I can hardly spoil the festive atmosphere by announcing that I surprised my future husband in bed with another woman this morning. Perhaps I can invent a sudden lurid illness for him.'

'Why not have dinner with me?' Rhodri asked unexpectedly.

Sarah stared at him in surprise. 'That's extraordinarily kind of you, but you don't have to carry your knight-errantry that far! You've already endured my outpourings and provided me with transport——'

'And I think it only fair that you should reward me by spending the evening with me,' he said promptly.

The idea was alluring, and the more Sarah considered it the more she liked it, but she shook her head regretfully. 'My family would think it odd.'

'Not if I say I bullied you into it—and I am an old friend of your brother's.'

You also happen to be lord of the manor, too, thought Sarah, which my mother would probably find reason enough.

'I don't know, Rhodri——' she began doubtfully.

'It's only a meal,' Rhodri laughed, his eyes dancing behind the dark lenses as he cast a sidelong glance at Sarah's face. 'I'm not proposing any droit de seigneur or anything.'

'As Rhia's the bride, not me, it hardly applies.' She looked at him curiously. 'Why are you doing all this?'

He shrugged. 'No reason in particular—let's say Friday is my day for rescuing damsels in distress.'

Sarah said no more as they left the bypass and turned into the town, leaving it almost immediately as Rhodri negotiated the car over the narrow hump-backed bridge spanning the River / Monnow, passing through the thirteenth-century gateway that guarded it before turning off on the road for Cwmderwen. She felt her spirits sinking as the powerful car ate up the short distance, and long before she felt ready to face the reunion with her family she was home. Rhodri turned the Porsche in through the familiar white gateway and halted it on the semicircle of gravel that bisected the lawn. Sarah's eyes stung as she looked at the old house, which was beautiful and infinitely satisfying to the eye. It was long and low, the rose-beige stone of the lower walls contrasting with the white plaster and black timbers of the upper half, the rust-red roof interspersed with the gables of the latticed bedroom windows. Two willows bent in graceful feathery fronds either side of the porch, where the black front door stood open.

For a moment Sarah knew panic, then Rhodri's strong, warm hand grasped hers as a sudden stream of people emerged from the house. Sarah's parents hurried out, smiling, followed at speed by the short, sturdy figure of Mari-Sîan, and, more indolently, by the willowy grace of Rhia's slender shape. Rhodri got out of the car and went round to help Sarah, as the Rev. Glyn Morgan came towards them hands outstretched, his eyes, the same distinctive blue as his daughters', regarding the arrivals with warm welcome mixed with some mystification. Sarah went to meet her parents on leaden feet, aware in some hyper-alert way of the expression on all four Morgan faces. There was an incredulous dawning hope on her mother's vivacious, still youthful face, Mari-Sîan was blatantly agog and Rhia—Rhia had eyes only for Sarah, a watchful look in the beautiful eyes before she schooled her face into the misty, enigmatic smile known to everyone who watched commercial television.

'Darling!' Mrs Morgan enfolded Sarah in loving arms, then held her away to look at her. 'How elegant you are!' She gave an uncertain smile at Sarah's escort, who stood back, his hair gleaming in the still bright sunlight.

'Hello, Mother, Father. I'm a bit early I'm afraid.' Sarah glanced at Rhodri and smiled. 'Rhodri here——'

He stepped forward and slid his arm round her waist.

'Good evening Mrs Morgan, Rector. Hello, Rhia,

Mari-Sîan.' He looked down possessively into Sarah's still face. 'I'm the surprise Sarah promised you.'

The ensuing half-hour was one Sarah lived through with difficulty. Rhodri held her in a grip of iron as Mrs Morgan embraced them both with rapture, then Glyn Morgan wrung Rhodri's hand with unabashed fervour, detaching Sarah from her mother to kiss her fondly as Mari-Sîan joined in the congratulations and Rhia enveloped Rhodri in a cloud of Calèche as she kissed him, smiling her famous smile before turning to Sarah in admiration.

'Congratulations, little sister—what a return for the prodigal daughter; in a spectacular car and with the squire in tow!'

The Rector turned to his eldest daughter in mild reproof.

'Hardly the prodigal, Rhiannon. Sarah comes home regularly, if not as frequently as we would like. It just happens that lately your visits never seem to coincide.'

'Come in the house,' urged Mrs Morgan. 'We must drink to this wonderful news. We're expecting Gareth and his family any minute—he'll be so delighted, Rhodri! Who would have thought that one day you and Sarah would come together like this.' She drew Rhodri with her, leaving Sarah to follow with Mari-Sîan and Rhia as her father hurried into the house to pour out sherry in celebration.

Mari-Sîan, forthright as usual, grinned at Sarah, her eyes mischievous behind her large, gold-rimmed spectacles as they studied both her sisters' faces, at once so much alike and yet subtly different.

'Got to hand it to you, Sal, that's the neatest bit of scene-stealing I've ever seen. Hard luck, Rhia.'

Sarah stopped in her tracks, just outside the door, and looked at Rhia levelly. 'I never intended it like that, Rhia. You may find that hard to believe, but it's the truth.'

Rhia leaned against the ancient, studded door, slender and elegant in white trousers and a pink silk shirt, her hands thrust in her pockets as she looked at Sarah, her jewel-like eyes guardedly amused.

'I'll believe you, darling, thousands wouldn't. Now hadn't we better go inside and drink a toast or two? God knows we've plenty to drink to.'

The familiar smell of wax polish, flowers and the faint hint of incense that always clung to her father, enveloped Sarah in the nostalgic aroma of home as she followed Rhia and Mari-Sîan into the comfortable, shabby elegance of the Rectory drawing room, and accepted a glass of sherry from her father, avoiding his questioning look as she took her drink across the room in response to Rhodri's beckoning hand. He stood, completely at home and relaxed, talking to her mother in front of the fireplace, answering eager questions with a mendacious ease that Sarah envied.

'I was coming out of Lord's cricket ground one day, and who should I bump into but little Miss Morgan here,' he was saying. He slid his arm round Sarah's waist again, bringing her close with such a look of possession in his smiling grey eyes that Mrs Morgan positively quivered with appreciation. 'Of course I didn't recognise her at once, her face has changed quite a bit, and the long hair was missing, but there was that unmistakable moment of recognition, and I knew I'd met my Waterloo.'

Rhia looked at him in undisguised amusement. 'How utterly romantic, Rhodri—love at first sight. A rarity these days.'

He bowed gracefully, his fingers still biting into Sarah's ribs through the silk of her blouse, as if to emphasize that all this was really happening.

'Nothing in the world to beat it, Rhia.' Rhodri raised his glass and smiled at everyone in general. 'And now may I propose a toast to tomorrow's bride; surely the most beautiful ever to be married at St David's church in all its not inconsiderable history. To Rhia.'

'To Rhia,' everyone echoed, Sarah flooded with relief as the attention shifted to her sister, who accepted it all as her natural due, chatting gaily to Rhodri about London and mutual acquaintances, while Mrs Morgan drew Sarah aside and gazed at her in tremulous wonder.

'To think that this was the surprise you talked about, my love. However did you manage to keep the secret?'

Sarah smiled weakly, feeling sick. 'It wasn't easy, Mother. Sorry to spring it on you like that.'

'Where's your ring?' chimed in Mari-Sîan, lifting Sarah's hand.

'I'm hoping that one of the family rings will please Sarah,' intervened Rhodri instantly. 'If not I'll buy her whatever she wants, of course.' He smiled warmly at Sarah. 'Now walk me to the car, darling, I'd better get back.'

'Oh, but you'll come back to dinner, Rhodri,' said Mrs Morgan immediately. 'Just a cold meal tonight, but Sir Charles will be here later with his two little girls, and Gareth and his wife, of course——'

'I'm sorry, Mrs Morgan,' said Rhodri hastily. 'I'm afraid I want to steal Sarah from you this evening. I hope you'll forgive me.'

'Of course, Rhodri. At least have another drink.' Glyn Morgan topped up Rhodri's glass. 'How is Lady Marian? Well, I hope?'

'Visiting my aunt in Ireland, sir. She doesn't enjoy the best of health these days, and her doctor advised a change and a rest. I'm keeping an eye on things in her absence.' The two men became engrossed in matters concerning the Lloyd-Ellis estate, and Sarah turned to her sister.

'Tell me about your bridegroom, Rhia.' Sarah was glad to divert the conversation away from herself. 'What's he like?'

Rhia subsided into one of the worn brocade armchairs and handed her glass to Mari-Sîan. 'Get me about another teaspoonful, darling, will you?' Her eyes met Sarah's very directly. 'He's Hadley Electronics, and rather wealthy. He's forty, a widower, very attractive in a rather austere, misleading way and I'm—fond of him. Very fond.'

'How will you enjoy being a stepmother?' asked Sarah

curiously. 'I find it hard to envisage you with a ready-made family.'

Rhia's eyes dropped to the huge diamond solitaire she was turning round and round on her engagement finger. 'The prospect frightens me not a little, I'll admit, but I intend to do my utmost to make a go of it. The girls are young, five and six respectively, and their mother died when Emma was born. Kate doesn't really remember her mother at all, so they don't seem to resent me.' There was an odd, fierce look in the eyes she raised to Sarah's. 'I want nothing to spoil my marriage if I can possibly prevent it.'

'Why should it?' Sarah returned the look steadily for a moment then turned to Mari-Sîan. 'How did A-levels go?'

Mari-Sîan made a face. 'Pretty gruesome. Who *likes* exams? I might just scrape the grades I want.'

There was mutual laughter from both Sarah and Rhia. While not as beautiful as either of her sisters, Mari-Sîan had been blessed with a mind like a computer, and had already passed her fourth-term Oxbridge entrance exam. The A-level results were a mere formality as far as her headmistress's predictions were concerned, but in spite of this Mari-Sîan hated to be considered clever, secretly longing for the sylph-like silhouette and flawless face she would have traded any day for her own razor-sharp brain and more generous proportions.

Rhodri finally managed to take his leave of Sarah's parents, and she went out to the car with him, keeping silent until they reached the Porsche.

'What on earth possessed you?' she hissed, not daring to glare at Rhodri in case they were overlooked.

'Let's sit in the car for a moment,' he said pacifyingly, and opened the door for her. Sarah slid inside quickly.

'Do you realise just what you've embroiled us in?' she demanded hotly when he was seated beside her. Rhodri half-turned towards her, and laid his arm along the back of her seat.

'Sarah, I swear the words came out quite involun-

tarily—honestly.' He brushed a straying lock of fair hair
back from his forehead, a rueful look in his eyes as he
took off the sunglasses. 'You emerged from the car like a
martyr going to the stake when your family appeared,
and suddenly I just had to make things easy for you.'

Sarah just looked at him, shaking her head slowly, a
reluctant smile dawning in her eyes as she sighed
hopelessly.

'Easy! We are now "betrothed", if you'll pardon the
expression; in the eyes of my family at least, Rhodri
Lloyd-Ellis, and shall have to remain that way until after
the wedding. Then our sudden whirlwind romance will
have to whirl to an end as quickly as it began.' Her voice
quavered as she stopped speaking, and to her consternation tears spilled from her hot eyes, splashing down on the
silk of her blouse. She turned her head away sharply in
embarrassment. 'Oh Lord, I am sorry,' she choked.

Rhodri gave a muffled exclamation and pulled her
close so that her head lay on his shoulder.

'Don't cry, for God's sake, Sarah. I was trying to save
you misery, not cause it.' He gave a hunted glance
towards the house and drew her closer. 'I see a face in the
window—they think I can't keep my hands off you.' He
bent his head and kissed her quivering mouth lightly.
Sarah's wet eyes flew open her tears drying as he drew
back slightly, his face alight with sudden laughter. 'Might
as well keep up appearances,' he murmured, and kissed
her again.

Sarah pushed him away firmly, sniffing prosaically.
'No need to overdo it. Do I look a sight?'

He nodded, grinning. 'A sight for sore eyes, love. You'd
better go in. Don't forget, we met near the Underground
in St John's Wood, and I live in Little Venice, by the
way.'

Sarah smiled crookedly. 'Oh what a tangled web and
all that. Let's hope we don't trip ourselves up in the
strands.' She got out of the car and leaned through the
window. 'I haven't said thank you. It was a very quixotic
thing to do, but very sweet.'

Rhodri shrugged this aside. 'Let's say it just seemed like a good idea at the time. I'll be back for you about eight.'

'I'll be ready.'

Sarah stood looking after the car as it turned out of the drive to negotiate the dangerous blind bend beyond, then went dispiritedly back into the house to run the gauntlet of her family's curiosity and excitement. After only a few minutes of quick-fire questions from her mother and Mari-Sîan Sarah called a halt, aware of Rhia's silence.

'Shall we give it a rest,' she suggested. 'This is Rhia's wedding, after all, so let's forget about Rhodri and me. I want to hear all the bridal details—and if you can rustle up a cup of tea and a sandwich or something I'd be grateful. I shan't get any dinner until at least nine by the sound of it.'

Mrs Morgan went off at once to the kitchen while her husband slipped out through the back garden to the church, and Rhia gave Sarah the rundown on the wedding arrangements. Apparently the Rectory would be overflowing that night. Sir Charles was putting up in Monmouth, but his small daughters were sleeping in the tiny room next to Sarah's.

'Not that you're sleeping in your own room,' chimed in Mari-Sîan. 'You're slumming it with me in mine, Rhia and her wedding dress are occupying yours, Gareth, Jane, Davina and Eiry are all crammed into Rhia's room and Aunt Clarice is arriving later, and she's in the guest room. Mam didn't like to put anyone in with her.'

'Aunt Clarice!' Sarah looked in horror at Rhia who nodded in resignation. 'Thank goodness I'm dining out.'

'Lucky old you,' said Rhia dryly. 'Father insisted I invite her. The trouble is that she's so deaf, poor old thing.'

'And no doubt still as hideously forthright?'

'Oh yes,' said Mari-Sîan with relish. 'Think of her reaction when she hears about you and Rhodri Lloyd-Ellis.'

Sarah quailed at the prospect, then got up as her

mother called from the kitchen. 'Come on, let's comfort ourselves with some carbohydrates.' She glanced at Rhia's slender figure. 'Not counting calories any more are you?'

Rhia shook her head with a blissful sigh and stood up, stretching. 'No need any more. I've given up starving myself for the camera's sake. Charles would like me to gain a few pounds.'

'Have some of mine,' offered Mari-Sîan gloomily.

Elizabeth Morgan looked on with a glow of satisfaction as her three daughters sat down at the kitchen table and tucked in to moist dark fruit cake and several cups of tea, her eyes lingering longest on Sarah, whose short cropped hair stood out in contrast to the long, luxuriant manes of the other two. Before the meal was over a car sounded outside in the drive and Dr Gareth Morgan and his wife Jane arrived, plus two small girls and a large excited golden labrador in an uproar of greetings and barking.

'Did you have to bring Juno as well?' demanded Mrs Morgan, her eyes everywhere as the lively dog skidded on the polished wood floor of the hall.

'Oh Mam! You wouldn't have me put her in kennels— you know she pines.' Gareth, large, dark and unrepentant, kissed his mother and sisters with enthusiasm, bellowing at the dog, issuing instructions to his wife and children on unpacking the car, and simultaneously demanding all the latest news from Rhia and Sarah, gratifyingly surprised when he heard about Rhodri. Before the explanations were finished the sound of another car could be heard outside and Rhia cried 'Charles!', rushing out to meet her bridegroom as he emerged from the Daimler in the drive, followed by two fair little girls who hung back shyly as their father, a tall, slimly built man with grey-streaked dark hair, enfolded Rhia in an embrace that made no bones about his feelings for her. Rhia bent to kiss the two wide-eyed children, and turned to the rest of her family, holding Emma and Kate by the hand as she smiled up at Charles Hadley with a look that plainly reciprocated his feelings.

'Charles, come and meet the rest of my family,' she said happily. 'Look, everyone, these are Emma and Kate, my new little girls. Don't you think I'm lucky?'

Rhia had always been lucky, thought Sarah later. She was dressing for her evening with Rhodri, somewhat cramped by the confines of Mari-Sîan's room, which only just allowed for the extra camp-bed squeezed into it. Rhia had always sailed through life with ease, floating like a butterfly where others floundered, achieving her goals without apparent effort. The accident that proved so costly to Sarah in various ways had left Rhia unmarked, and it was a wonder to Sarah that this successful, brilliant marriage had not occurred long before Rhia reached the age of twenty-six. For years Sarah had avoided thinking about Rhia at all, almost afraid of her own feelings, but seeing her today with the rather vulnerable look on her face as she looked up at Charles Hadley, Sarah had experienced an unexpected fellow-feeling. Zipping up the black-dotted white crêpe-de-chine dress bought some time ago for dining with Rupert, Sarah screwed her head round to look at her back view, then brushed her hair and ran her fingers through the front, ruffling it across her forehead. She stood still, looking at her face in the mirror, struck by the thought that fate was a bit haphazard in dealing out the experiences allotted to each person in a life time. Today Sarah felt she'd run the gamut of every emotion she would ever be likely to feel again—and the day was by no means over.

Mari-Sîan came in and sat down gingerly on the camp-bed, looking at Sarah with envy.

'Gorgeous dress. You're into black and white rather a lot these days.'

'M'm. I suppose I am.' Sarah threaded small turquoise-studded silver hoops through her earlobes and decided she would do.

'It's like a mad-house down there,' observed her sister, and sprayed herself with some of Sarah's perfume. 'You're sneaky, going out. With any luck you'll even miss seeing Aunt Clarice if you come home late enough.'

'I'll keep that in mind. How are Kate and Emma coping with all this fuss, Mari-Sîan, they seemed a bit overwhelmed when they arrived—probably the over-abundance of Morgans everywhere, poor little things.' Sarah felt a little sorry for the fair, timid little girls, so unlike Gareth's dark, red-cheeked daughters, lively creatures who appeared more mature then the other two.

'When last seen they were tearing round the orchard at the back with Eiry, Davina and dog, and firmly resisting all attempts to capture them for supper and bed.' Mari-Sîan yawned hugely. 'The four of them should make cute bridesmaids.'

'What's your dress like?'

'Very plain. Kingfisher-blue linen, with dark blue strappy sandals, and a sort of pill-box thing as a hat.'

Sarah looked at her in surprise. 'Aren't you a bridesmaid then, love?'

Mari-Sîan shook her head.

'Rhia asked, of course, but as you wouldn't it seemed best if I didn't either. Besides,' she added, making a face, 'I would have looked horrendous in frilled silk net tied up with pink ribbons, now, wouldn't I? As it is the kiddy-winkies will look gorgeous, I will look at least reasonably slim in my nice plain dress and you, no doubt, have some stunning outfit that will knock Cwmderwen's eyes out.'

Sarah gave her sister a wry look. 'Those myopic eyes of yours see far too much at times.'

'I'm wearing contact lenses tomorrow, Sal, so everyone can get bowled over by the concerted effect of the Morgan eyes in toto.' Mari-Sîan jumped up to look out of the window at the sound of an approaching car. 'On your bike, Sal, young Lochinvar is come out of the west!'

Despite feeling distinctly guilty about deserting her family on her first night home Sarah enjoyed her evening. Rhodri took her to an out-of-the-way inn which provided a plain but excellent dinner, and the only awkward moment came when he insisted on lending Sarah a sapphire ring rifled from his mother's jewel-box in the safe at the Court. Sarah was very unwilling to take responsibility for such a valuable piece of jewellery, especially in Lady Marian's absence, but Rhodri was insistent, with the unanswerable logic that without a ring their harmless little charade would lack authenticity. He assured her that the ring was fully insured, and of no sentimental value, and Sarah gave in, finding Rhodri's company soothing and undemanding as they talked together on a variety of subjects, thoughts of Rupert kept rigidly under lock and key in her mind.

It was well past midnight by the time she eventually stole quietly through the front door of the Rectory, hoping to get upstairs without meeting anyone. The house was in darkness, except for a dim light in the drawing room, and to Sarah's surprise Rhia appeared in the doorway and pulled her into the deserted room and closed the door carefully.

'What are you doing up?' demanded Sarah in an undertone. 'You should be in bed getting your beauty-sleep; not that you need it.'

Rhia pulled Sarah down beside her on the familiar old brocade sofa and looked into her face searchingly.

'I wanted to talk to you alone—we shan't get another chance.' She ran the tip of her tongue over her lips and looked away. 'Things have never been the same between us, have they? Not since the accident.'

Sarah stiffened, her arm taut beneath Rhia's touch.

'Oh Rhia,' she sighed. 'It was a long time ago, and we're not the same people now that we were then. I like to think I've matured at least a little.'

Rhia withdrew her hand, her face sad. 'The biggest change is the barrier you've built between yourself and the rest of us, Sarah. Mari-Sîan is the only one you respond to normally.'

Sarah shrugged, looking down at her hands. 'She was the only one who ever behaved normally about the whole business. I suppose she was only a child, but it never mattered to her—I was still Sal, no matter how I looked or how I'd behaved. It was different with Mother and Father. I never imagined how hard it would be to cope with forgiveness.' She looked up to meet Rhia's eyes. 'Perhaps you can understand that.'

Rhia nodded sombrely. 'Yes, Sarah, I can. If you knew how often I've wished one could turn the clock back to some time before that wretched party——'

Sarah put out a hand to cover Rhia's. 'Don't Rhia.' She smiled steadily. 'I think it's time we did put the clock back, pretend the whole thing never happened. God knows I'd like to, and concentrate on the future.'

'Amen to that,' said Rhia fervently, her hand clasping Sarah's convulsively. 'I do so want tomorrow to be a happy day, Sarah, with no shadows spoiling it for you or for me. Is that possible?'

'Yes, of course.' Sarah's voice was husky.

Rhia suddenly caught sight of the ring Sarah wore.

'So that's the ring Rod gave you! Very nice indeed.' She leaned forward, hesitated a moment, then kissed Sarah's cheek. 'Be happy. Now I think it's time for bed.'

As they left the room Rhia whispered, 'By the way, there was a phone call for you tonight, I answered it.'

'Really?' Sarah's heart gave a great lurch.

'Your literary lion, Rupert Clare. He asked if you'd arrived safely.'

'What did you tell him?'

'I just said you had, and you were out having dinner with your fiancé. Goodnight Sarah, sleep well.'

CHAPTER FOUR

RHIA's parting instruction was impossible to follow. Far into the night Sarah cried silent, scalding tears into her pillow, neither Rhodri's generous gesture nor her improved relationship with Rhia enough to banish the thoughts of Rupert that came flooding back the moment she was in bed. The effort of keeping her grief from the slumbering Mari-Sîan, and the agony of reliving the scene in Rupert's bedroom over and over again hardly made for the most peaceful of nights, and Sarah woke at first light after only the briefest of dozes, feeling headachey and utterly disinclined to face the day she knew was in store.

She was not in the least surprised to find the day clear and sunny. Rhia gave and expected perfection, and the weather was apparently prepared to keep to the rules. Mari-Sîan came to early with a lot of grumbling and stretching, and crawled blindly out of bed, groping for her spectacles and barking her shins as she negotiated the narrow space between the beds.

'Going to the bathroom,' she mumbled, and went out of the room, returning a few minutes later with her face washed, and a less jaundiced look on life.

'Have a nice evening?' she asked, and crawled back into her makeshift bed, her face expectant.

'Very nice.' Sarah obligingly supplied the necessary information about the food, and got out of bed to display the ring.

'Old-fashioned, but *very* nice,' was Mari-Sîan's verdict. She gave a sharp look at her sister's wan face. 'You don't exactly look like the first breath of spring, though, Sal. Headache?'

'Yes,' answered Sarah casually, shrugging into her dressing gown. 'Too much wine, I expect. I'd better get moving before Aunt Clarice hogs the bathroom.'

'Of course, you don't know. She never turned up last night. She rang to say she could get a lift today as long as the driver—the bloke next door—could come to the reception. Mother was translated with joy. Aunt Clarice was welcome to bring Jack the Ripper as far as she was concerned as long as he took Auntie back home afterwards.' Mari-Sîan pulled up the covers with a yawn as Sarah smiled despite her heavy head and went off to the bathroom to take some aspirin and perform some rapid ablutions before the rest of the family were astir. In red linen trousers and white shirt she stole downstairs to the kitchen to make herself some restorative tea, to find her father just coming in from a walk with Gareth's dog.

'Good morning, Sarah.' Glyn Morgan embraced his daughter, kissing her cheek. 'You're an early bird. Did you have a pleasant evening?' He looked at her more closely. 'You look a little peaked, cariad.' He turned away to fill a dish with water for the panting Juno.

'I'm never at my best in the mornings.' Sarah filled the kettle and put out cups and saucers on the table as her father sat down, a contented look on his scholarly handsome face as his eyes followed Sarah about the big, familiar room that was already filled with early morning sunlight.

'Did you have a good meal?' he asked.

'Very good. I felt very guilty to be sneaking away, when it must have been like the tower of Babel here at home.' Sarah poured boiling water on the tea-leaves her mother preferred to tea-bags, and set the big brown pot to brew on the back of the Aga stove. 'What can I get you to eat—bacon, eggs?'

Glyn Morgan had long since given up eating a cooked breakfast, but at the prospect of having his daughter to himself for a while he assented promptly on the condition that Sarah joined him. Her headache was fading already, and to her surprise the thought of an unaccustomed hearty breakfast was quite welcome, in vivid contrast to the solitary cup of black coffee gulped in the flat before her day's work with Rupert. Stop it, she told herself savagely, forget Rupert, blot him out of your mind, pretend he never existed, and with determination she turned away to switch on the grill and take a heavy frying pan from a cupboard, moving swiftly from refrigerator to cooker with eggs, bacon, mushrooms, and finally a plastic bowl she produced with a smile as she swung round to her father.

'Laver bread, Dad—would you like some?'

His eyes twinkled, hiding the secret stab of joy felt at her reversion to the 'Dad' of childhood.

'Your mother always gets hold of some when Gareth's coming. Shall we both steal a little before he scoffs the lot?'

Sarah chuckled and spooned some of the oozing black seaweed mixture into the bacon fat in a small frying pan, broke eggs into another and turned the bacon under the grill while her father laid the table and cut bread. They both sat down to a piping hot breakfast seconds later, Sarah secretly amazed that she looked forward to it with anticipation, considering the night she'd spent.

'I haven't eaten a breakfast like this for ages.' Her mouth was frankly full as she buttered a piece of bread.

'Neither have I, to be honest,' confessed her father boyishly. 'It tastes marvellous.'

'I shouldn't be hungry at all,' said Sarah ruefully. 'We ate quite late last night.'

'You're happy, Sarah?' asked her father quietly.

Feeling like the worst of hypocrites Sarah smiled brightly and held out her hand for him to admire her ring, nodding her head in answer to his question. The chiming of the church clock interrupted them, and Sarah jumped up to pour tea.

'Six-thirty.' Glyn Morgan smiled at Sarah. 'Our peace will soon be shattered. Oh, by the way, there was a phone call for you last night from your author. Rhia answered it.'

'Yes, I know. She waited up to tell me when I got home.'

The Rector looked warily at Sarah, then relaxed at the

untroubled expression on her face, obviously pleased that his daughters appeared to have ended the rift between them.

'Nothing important, I gather?'

'No. Rupert—Mr Clare—merely wanted to know if I had arrived safely.' To her annoyance colour rose in Sarah's face, and she jumped up to clear the table, washing up swiftly while her father dried the dishes and re-laid the table.

'Whatever are you doing up so early?' Mrs Morgan came into the room with an accusing look on her face. 'Not you, Glyn, of course, you always are, but I hoped you'd have a bit of a rest, Sarah, you look very tired.'

'I woke up and that was that,' said Sarah blythely and pushed her mother into a chair. 'Now sit there like a good girl while Dad pours you a cup of tea and I cook a nice breakfast for you, just like the one we had.'

'Sarah's right, Beth. You've been working yourself to a standstill over this wedding. A good breakfast will set you up for the day.' Glyn Morgan laid a firm hand on his wife's shoulder and kept her in her chair. She laughed and protested, but gave in and enjoyed the meal Sarah cooked for her, her eyes on her daughter in wonder. With one of her mother's shiny plastic aprons over her shirt and slacks, Sarah looked almost like the schoolgirl she had once been, apart from the slight shadows beneath her eyes. Mari-Sîan was the next to arrive, only too glad of Sarah's offer of breakfast, promising faithfully to wash up afterwards.

'Keep some laver bread for Gareth, mind,' warned Mrs Morgan.

'*I* don't want any of the beastly stuff.' Mari-Sîan shuddered.

'Perhaps Rhia would like breakfast in bed,' suggested Sarah, 'After all, she is the bride.'

'That would be nice.' Mrs Morgan cast a grateful look at Sarah. 'What about the little girls?'

'I expect they'd prefer their breakfast with Eiry and Davina when they get up.' Her husband smiled. 'They thawed out considerably last night after you left, Sarah. They got on very well with the other two—I think Juno here broke the ice.' He stroked the dog, who laid her head on his knee, gazing up at him with melting adoration.

'What happens to Emma and Kate while Rhia and Charles are on their honeymoon?' asked Sarah.

'Jane and Gareth are having them to stay.' Mrs Morgan smiled comfortably. 'They'll be well looked after there.'

The question of Rhia's breakfast was settled by her arrival a moment later, hand in hand with Emma and Kate. She looked far from bridal in jeans, with her hair in a plait down her back and her face scrubbed and free of make-up. The two children broke away from her in delight as Juno wagged her tail and made noises of welcome, submitting to their petting and stroking and dispelling any shyness.

'I was all ready to bring you breakfast in bed,' said Sarah after the chorus of good mornings was over.

Rhia looked startled.

'Were you indeed! How noble. I hate to spoil your burst of virtue, but black coffee and orange-juice is my limit in the mornings.'

'Not *this* morning,' said her mother firmly. 'You must have something inside you when you float down the aisle.' She bent to talk to Emma and Kate. 'Will you have bacon and egg, my lovelies? Yes? That's the way.'

'Come on then, Rhia,' said Mari-Sîan. 'Sit down and let Sarah get on with it—she seems to have her chef's hat on.'

'It must be the ring.' Rhia smiled mischievously as Mrs Morgan pounced on Sarah, taking her hand and scolding volubly.

'Fancy frying bacon with a beautiful ring like that on! You must be mad, child!'

'I'm afraid to take it off in case I lose it!' Sarah shooed them away and returned to her impromptu role as caterer, finding she was enjoying herself, even extending her labours to include her large brother and his family when they appeared, waving away her capable sister-in-law's protests and insisting on her sitting down to be waited on, as a rare treat. There was a general laugh halfway through the meal when Jane jumped to her feet automatically at the sound of the telephone, a sheepish look on her face as she sat down again.

'You're not at home now, darling,' said Gareth fondly. 'That's more likely to be one of Dad's parishioners than one of my patients, thank God.'

The Rector returned from the hall with a beckoning finger in Sarah's direction and she hurried from the room, thinking it might be Rhodri.

'You're up early,' she said cheerfully into the receiver.

'What the hell did you expect?' The cold drawl in her ear was unmistakable. The tiny hairs stood proud all along her spine as Sarah stiffened, her heart thumping.

'I have nothing to say to you——' she began icily, but Rupert broke in.

'But I have a bloody great deal to say to you, Sarah! What in God's name is all this about a fiancé—who is he? What the devil are you up to?'

'I refuse to say a word——'

'Now you just listen to me, woman!'

'I will not! And don't call me woman.' Sarah was trembling with rage.

'Sarah, please——' Rupert's husky voice suddenly had a note of pleading never heard in it before, but she ignored it.

'I don't want to talk to you, Rupert. Not now, nor at any time in the future; ever! Goodbye.' Sarah slammed the phone down and stood in the cool hall with her eyes shut and her fists clenched, the chimes of the clock as it struck nine reverberating through her body like hammer strokes. She opened her eyes to see Rhodri standing in the open doorway with a large box. He dumped it on the floor and held out his arms. Sarah flew into them, leaning her head against his chest as his arms closed round her like bastions of comfort and protection.

'Clare?' he muttered against her hair.

Sarah nodded blindly, breathing deeply, then withdrew from his arms as the kitchen door opened and Mrs Morgan emerged, smiling with pleasure as she saw Rhodri.

'Rhodri, good morning. Come in, come in, we're lingering over a very protracted breakfast. Sarah's been at the stove since the crack of dawn, she deserves a rest and some coffee.'

'Good morning, Mrs Morgan. I've brought a present for Rhia.' Rhodri kept an arm firmly round Sarah and took her with him as he joined the rest of the family in the kitchen, Gareth springing up in welcome and shooing the children outside into the garden with the dog to make more room.

'Sit down, Rod, have some coffee. Or do you fancy some bacon and laver bread?' Gareth gave a sly grin. 'Sarah here has been cooking for all of us this morning. I'm sure she'd include you if you twist her arm!'

Rhodri shook his head, smiling at everyone. 'Not for me thanks. Good morning, sir.' He greeted Sarah's father, then Jane and Mari-Sîan, finally smiling at Rhia. 'And how are you this morning, Rhia? Blooming, if appearances are anything to go by. I've brought you a present.'

Rhia's eyes widened. 'But Lady Marian sent us a beautiful Georgian tea-caddy, Rod, there was really no need for you to give something too.'

He laughed and released Sarah's cold hand to get the large box from the hall, revealing a brass-banded oak wine cooler, and Rhia embraced him with gratitude, smiling at Sarah in apology as she gave Rhodri a smacking kiss.

Rhodri stayed only long enough to reassure himself that Sarah had fully recovered her composure, and shortly after he left Mrs Morgan, Rhia and Mari-Sîan departed for the hairdressers. As Jane was quite happy to oversee the children Sarah went with her father along the familiar path through the back garden and the creaking

postern gate into the churchyard. The church of St David
nestled in a fold in the hills, looking out over the verdant,
rolling countryside of Gwent as it had done from the time
of its first incumbent in 1340. Sarah stopped for a
moment to take in the picture the ancient building made,
gilded by the morning sunlight. The church was small,
with a fore-shortened square tower, the stone base topped
with black-and-white timbering and surmounted by a
simple wrought-iron cross. Some of the gravestones
nearest the church were old, with indecipherable dates
and names. Others farther afield were contemporary, and
one sadly recent enough to lack the headstone that would
shortly mark the final resting place of its occupant. Sarah
followed her father into the porch, running a hand
lovingly over the inscription surrounding the heavy,
weathered door. 'Here the rich and the poor meet
together. The Lord is the Maker of them all.' She sighed,
breathing in the smell of incense, ancient wood and
much-used books, the sheer age that was an integral part
of the tapestry of her childhood. Her footsteps echoed on
the stone flags before she knelt in the nearest pew and
said a prayer for the first time in years. As she stood again
Sarah looked with pleasure and appreciation at the
flowers decorating the church, recognising her mother's
deft hand in the delicate arrangements of roses,
honeysuckle and stephanotis. A frown creased her
forehead suddenly.

'Dad!'

Her father turned from the altar. 'What is it, cariad?'

Sarah looked at him with troubled eyes. 'I know it's
none of my business, but—well, isn't this wedding costing
you a lot of money? I know we all joke about Mother's
private means, but there's still Mari-Sîan to put through
college. I—I wondered if you'd allow me to contribute in
some way?'

Glyn Morgan came down the aisle and put an arm
round Sarah. 'A very lovely thought, but it really isn't
necessary. In the first place your mother's private means,
carefully invested, really do exist, by kind courtesy of the

money your grandfather left from his foundry. Without it
I would never have been able to continue here in this
beautiful backwater and occupy myself with the history of
this church all these years. I owe a great deal to your
mother.'

'Mother doesn't see it that way though, does she?'

'No. She never has.' He smiled fondly. 'Also, I must
confess that we've been allowed to foot the bill for very
little. Rhiannon insisted on standing the cost of the
reception herself, and has bought her own dress. Charles
is seeing to the wine, transport, flowers, etc., as is
customary, so as you see, Sarah, all I had to do was buy
Beth and Mari-Sîan a new dress each, and Rhiannon a
wedding present.'

Sarah felt reassured, and pleasantly surprised. 'Sorry to
poke my nose in like that,' she said awkwardly. 'I was just
a little concerned that's all. Now I'd best get back and do
something to my hair.'

Back at the house she found Jane supervising baths for
four rather grubby little bridesmaids, and volunteered to
do a stint of blow-drying on the young ladies, to her
sister-in-law's relief, who went off to get dressed in peace
while she had the chance. The rest of the morning passed
in a frenzy of last-minute preparations once Rhia
returned, looking exquisite with her hair looped into a
knot high on her head. Mrs Morgan and Mari-Sîan were
equally sleek about the head, but the former regarded
Sarah's flushed face and untidy hair with disapproval, as
she realised that here was one Morgan who was far from
being ready.

'Don't scold her, Mother,' said Jane swiftly. 'Sarah's
been doing the girls' hair for me. Come and see the
flowers, they put them in the pantry to keep fresh.'

Diverted, Mrs Morgan and Rhia went to inspect the
bouquets while Sarah flew to wash her hair and dry it
quickly, a daily occupation which took only ten minutes.

'I wish my hair was cut like that.' Mari-Sîan watched
from the other bed, eating a packet of crisps. 'I had to
have mine slicked back like this so that I could get my

hat on, but it'll never stay tidy. Yours looks great already.'

'It also costs a lot to keep it that way,' said Sarah and put her hairdryer away. 'It needs trimming every three weeks—sometimes I think I'll grow it again and save my money.'

Mari-Siân looked at the satin dress and jacket on a hanger outside the wardrobe, naked envy in her eyes.

'I must go on a diet—I'd give my soul to wear something like that.'

Sarah gave her a push, grinning. 'You'd better get into the dress you *are* wearing. I'll just see if Rhia needs any help while you change.'

Rhia was busy fastening her future stepdaughters into enchanting white net dresses with floating pink ribbons. Sarah helped them put on white satin ballet shoes and Rhia popped wreaths of pink and white roses on their heads, then stood back in satisfaction as the little girls smiled with endearing delight at their reflections. 'You look scrumptious,' said Rhia, kissing them both.

'Delicious,' agreed Sarah. 'Shall I take them downstairs Rhia? I think Eiry and Davina are ready.'

'Thanks, Sarah.' Rhia gestured towards the dress that hung from the old-fashioned clothes tree, the folds still protected by its wrappings. 'I'd rather not get into that until the last possible moment. What are you wearing?'

'A satin dress and jacket,' said Sarah casually, '*and* a hat, a fact which I hope you are registering with due respect. Anything else I can do, Rhia?'

'No thanks, love—see you in church!'

Sarah grinned and, hand in hand with Kate and Emma went downstairs to pass them over to Jane, who was keeping her own lively pair penned in the drawing room in an effort to keep the white dresses clean.

'Where's Juno?' whispered Kate suddenly, her face troubled.

'She's out in the garage for the time being, darling.' Jane smiled understandingly. 'Don't worry—we've put her bed in there, and her dinner and a bowl of water.'

Sarah went back upstairs to her mother's room and helped zip up her burgundy crêpe dress and give advice on the correct placing of the matching straw hat on Mrs Morgan's silvered dark hair, and eventually had to hurry over her own dressing. The thick satin was smooth and cool on her bare skin as she slid her arms into the jacket. She shivered momentarily, giving herself a wry smile in the mirror as she set the Graham Smith boater dead straight above her eyes, anchoring it securely with a pearl-headed hatpin to match the pendant pearls in her ears. How excited and happy she had been as she chose the expensive outfit, wanting to look as beautiful as possible for Rupert as well as doing credit to her family at the wedding. Sarah sighed, fiercely swallowing the unbidden lump that rose in her throat. Things could be a lot worse, she told herself resolutely. She had a more than presentable escort to the wedding, even if Rhodri was just a substitute, and even to her own eyes she had never looked more attractive or elegant than she did in her severely plain hat and beautifully cut dress. Closing her mind to thoughts of Rupert Sarah slid her feet into the wildly extravagant satin pumps and gathered up her gloves and purse, then went downstairs to endure the family group photograph which Gareth, resplendent in grey morning suit, insisted on taking once Sarah had found a hatpin for Mari-Sîan's blue velvet pill-box, which seemed to have taken on a life of its own. It was a relief when they were all installed in the church listening to Miss Gladys Rowlands playing softly on the organ, as she had done for every wedding in the church for the past thirty years. Sarah marvelled inwardly. All this was a long way from the sophisticated wedding she would have thought more in Rhia's line. There had been a battery of photographers at the gate, it was true, but the old church held only a limited number of guests, and it was hardly the usual type of wedding to make the pages of the glossy magazines. The corners of Sarah's mouth drooped a little as she wondered what Rupert would have made of it all. He was essentially a creature of pace and hassle and city pavements, scarcely the type to enjoy the rusticity of her present surroundings in Sarah's opinion. But then, what did she really know of him? she thought with cynicism. No doubt he would be like a chameleon, taking colour from wherever he found himself. Her abstraction was interrupted by a nudge from Mari-Sîan, and Sarah looked round to see Rhodri sliding into the pew behind them, wearing a pale beige suit of great elegance, a white gardenia in his lapel and the black eye safely concealed behind his dark glasses. Sarah returned his smile fleetingly, then looked across at Charles Hadley, who sat with his best man, tense and obviously nervous, as though this were his first marriage, which Sarah found rather endearing. There seemed to be something about weddings that scared men silly, she thought in amusement, wondering if it were the mere ceremony itself, or the prospect of future bondage that caused the terror.

Shortly afterwards Miss Rowlands struck the first sedate chords that heralded the bride. The Rev. Glyn Morgan stood at the altar steps, gazing down his church with a look of love and pride on his face as his son escorted his eldest daughter down the aisle. For a moment Sir Charles stood motionless, ramrod stiff with eyes straight ahead, then some inner compulsion seemed to turn him in Rhia's direction as she approached. The light in his eyes brought a sudden mist to Sarah's as she watched her sister, a vision of ethereal beauty in pearl-embroidered silk organza, smiling in tender radiance at her bridegroom, followed by four sweet, solemn neophytes, very much in awe of the occasion.

After the simple ceremony was over Sarah went with the rest of her family to the vestry, met Charles's cousin, the best man, and joined in much kissing and congratulating before the couple emerged to walk down the aisle to the triumphant strains of Lohengrin. Mari-Sîan, bringing up the rear of the procession with Sarah, muttered, 'Who's the man sitting alone at the back—look, near the font. He's on our side, must be one of Rhia's friends.'

Sarah looked past the colourful sea of fashionable hats and drew in a sharp breath, the colour draining from her face. There, large as life, in a dark striped suit with a red rose in his buttonhole, was Rupert Clare. His mouth was curved in an ironic smile, but his eyes were ice-cold and furious as they met Sarah's.

'What's up?' Mari-Sîan nudged Sarah to get her moving again. 'Do you know him?'

'He's my employer.' Sarah seethed inwardly. What the devil did Rupert think he was playing at? She moved unhurriedly past him with a cool little nod, acutely aware of her young sister's avid interest, glad when all the frenetic business of the wedding photographs enveloped them outside, as not only the official photographer, but a battery of press photographers had a field-day with their version of 'famous model and wealthy industrialist plump for romantic village wedding'.

Sarah stood rooted to the spot by panic as Rupert advanced towards her along the gravel path between the tombstones, his swagger even more arrogant than usual. She looked wildly for Rhodri, but he had been intercepted by friends in the crowd and Sarah was left on her own, to look back defiantly at Rupert as he stopped in front of her, his eyes raking her from head to toe as he inclined his head, the sun striking copper lights in his over-long brown hair.

'Good afternoon, Sarah. You look dauntingly *soignée*.' Receiving no response he turned to a deeply interested Mari-Sîan. 'And this must be yet another ravishing sister—quite a bevy of beauties, you Morgans.' He took Mari-Sîan's hand and smiled at her brilliantly, reducing her to jelly. 'I'm Rupert Clare.'

'I'm Mari-Sîan,' she breathed, her blue eyes like saucers. 'I had no idea *you* were coming!'

Rupert turned to the motionless Sarah with a suavely reproving smile.

'Sarah must have forgotten to mention it.'

'Silly of me,' murmured Sarah through stiff lips and looked along the path with relief. 'Here comes my mother, with my sister-in-law, and that's my brother Gareth, near the gate, talking to my—my fiancé, Rhodri Lloyd-Ellis.'

Rupert's cold green eyes followed her gesturing hand, rested for a moment on the man in question, then turned back to bore into hers like slivers of ice. 'I shall be interested to meet him,' he said, the faint menace in his voice feathering shivers up Sarah's spine as she turned almost wildly to her mother and Jane.

'Mother—such a surprise!' she cried with artificial gaiety. 'This is Rupert Clare, my employer. He happens to be in the area and came along to see the wedding.'

'Why Mr Clare! How extremely nice of you.' Mrs Morgan flushed quite pink with excitement. Rupert bowed over her hand and smiled with such charm Elizabeth Morgan fluttered visibly.

'It's no mystery as to where your daughters get their looks, Mrs Morgan. I'm very happy to meet you at last— I've heard so much about you.'

Sarah fumed impotently as Rupert turned his attention to Jane, then went on at some length on the beauty of the bride. Finally she interrupted to tell her mother that Gareth and her father were trying to attract her attention.

'So they are.' Mrs Morgan smiled warmly at Rupert. 'You will come along to the reception in Chepstow, Mr Clare, won't you? It's a buffet meal—one extra will be no problem. We'd be very pleased if you would.'

'How very kind, Mrs Morgan. I accept with pleasure. Perhaps Sarah will consent to navigate for me.' Rupert smiled challengingly in Sarah's direction.

'No!' she said involuntarily. 'I mean I'm travelling with Rhodri.' She took her sister by the arm and pushed her forward. 'Mari-Sîan will be only too delighted to show you the way.'

'Delighted' was hardly the word. Mari-Sîan was in seventh heaven at the idea of travelling to the reception in the white Rolls Corniche parked conspicuously in the lay-by near the church, not to mention having as escort a man not only gorgeous in her estimation but famous as well. Sarah's fervent wish to see them immediately on their way went unfulfilled, to her vexation. Rupert stood his ground as Rhodri could be seen making his way through the throng with purpose, both men quite plainly intent on making each other's acquaintance. At any other time Sarah would have revelled in the attention of two such attractive men in full view of the curious eyes of so many of Cwmderwen's inhabitants, but under the circumstances her nerve almost failed her. With the calm of desperation she introduced the two men to each other, her voice colourless, her smile polite, outwardly a model of cool composure, her eyes serene beneath the brim of the straw boater, giving no hint of the turmoil raging within.

'Wasn't it lucky Mr Clare happened to be in the neighbourhood in time for the wedding?' she heard herself saying inanely.

'Fortuitous in the extreme,' agreed Rhodri, unsmiling, and moved close to Sarah, his attitude openly protective.

Mari-Sîan watched, riveted, as Rupert directed a gleaming, glacial smile at Sarah, allowing it to fade deliberately as his eyes turned to Rhodri's hostile face. 'It's always been my intention to visit this part of the world—oddly enough unknown territory to me. And, of course, I've heard so much about Sarah's family I was eager to make their acquaintance. For some reason she's been more reticent about you.' He turned back to Sarah, his eyes suddenly outrageously intimate. 'After all, darling, you *did* invite me, if you remember.'

Sarah returned his look stonily. 'Yes, Rupert, I remember very well. I somehow assumed you'd had a change of heart.' With satisfaction she watched his eyes harden to chips of malachite, then turned away, catching sight of her brother's violently gesticulating arm. 'I rather fancy Gareth is getting a bit uptight—we really must make a move. I'll leave you in my sister's care, Rupert. You know the way, Mari-Sîan?'

Mari-Sîan nodded, her rounded face alight with anticipation.

'Come on, Mr Clare. I'm looking forward to my first ride in a Rolls.'

'Only the first of many, I'm certain, Mari-Sîan.' Rupert smiled down into her excited face and offered his arm. Enraptured, she took it and swept off with him in triumph beneath the admiring gaze of several schoolfriends, who were gathered at the lychgate to see the guests depart.

Once Sarah was in the hired Bentley in company with Jane, Gareth and Rhodri there was little opportunity for any private conversation, though Rhodri firmly took possession of her hand as they sat together in the back seat, silently offering his support.

'You didn't mention your boss was coming, Sal,' remarked Gareth.

'No,' said Sarah casually. 'I never thought for a moment he would.'

'Bit of a lad for the ladies, according to the press.' Gareth gave her a leer. 'Does he chase you round your desk?'

'Gareth!' Jane frowned blackly at her husband. 'Talking of the press there were a lot of photographers there today. It all went beautifully, didn't it?'

The others responded to this tactful diversion, and for the rest of the journey the conversation was confined to the events of the day, including the absence of Aunt Clarice, whose failure to turn up at the church was the source of much conjecture. When they reached the picturesque country club chosen for the reception Mrs Morgan was beginning to fret about it, but was obliged to stand in the receiving line as the guests arrived, her worries put aside for the moment amidst the kissing and congratulating as a radiant Rhia and her new husband received the best wishes of the smartly dressed guests waiting in line for the privilege. When Mari-Sîan came through the door with Rupert in tow Rhia shot a questioning look at Sarah as he was introduced. Sarah was too distant to hear what he was actually saying, but by the smiles of the people near by it was obviously something polished and witty—and facile, she added mentally, bitterness welling deep inside her at the disruption Rupert was causing her on a day she had been prepared to enjoy to the full after her reconciliation with Rhia.

Rhodri distracted her with a glass of champagne offered by a hovering waiter. 'Try to think of it as a joke, Sarah,' he said quietly, and smiled down at her in comfort. 'It's a rum go in some ways, you know. *He*'s the one with the invitation after all. *I*'m the interloper.'

'Not to me, Rhodri.' Sarah's response was quietly fierce. 'I admit I was dumbfounded when you sprang into the breach like that yesterday, but I'll always be grateful you did. I don't know how to thank you enough.'

He drank some champagne, apparently absorbed in his glass. 'Would you fear the worst if I said I could probably think of a way?'

'Wouldn't that be rather conceited of me?' She smiled back, her eyes dancing, aware with some sixth sense that though Rupert Clare was engaged in conversation with her father and Gareth, he was keeping track of every move she made.

'Not in the least.' Rhodri gave a look round the room, encompassing all the women present. 'Apart from Rhia—and being the bride she has a duty to look breathtaking—you are far and away the best-dressed *and* the most attractive woman in the room. I would be telling less than the truth if I said my intentions were, well, completely without thoughts of making love to you.'

Sarah drained her champagne, and accepted another glass from one of the constantly circling waiters, feeling rather cheered by his words.

'So it's not my well-informed mind that prompted your quixotic impulse yesterday?' Her lopsided smile brought Rhodri instantly nearer.

'The fact that its home is so stunning *is* an added bonus.' He grinned, and looked over her shoulder for a moment. 'Would you be interested in the fact that the famous author is fighting the urge to come over here and black my other eye?'

Sarah gave a delicate, cat-like little smile and slid a hand through Rhodri's arm, turning her face up towards him, eyes brimming with mischief beneath the severe hat-brim.

'Interested and delighted—neither of which I should be indelicate enough to admit, I know, but I'm only human. Are you sure you don't mind being made use of in this shameless fashion, Rhodri? You didn't know what you were letting yourself in for, did you?'

Rhodri put a hand over hers. 'I'm enjoying every minute of it so far—it has fringe benefits I never even thought of at the time.'

'Hey, you two, stop canoodling and circulate, for Pete's sake.' The carrying voice of Gareth interrupted Sarah and Rhodri, and most of the chattering knots of people near them. 'You can wait till your own wedding for all that.' He slapped Rhodri on the back, grinning at Sarah.

'If that's an example of your bedside manner,' she said acidly, 'I hope never to need your ministrations.'

Abruptly there was a diversion in the shape of a small, elderly lady, who appeared in the doorway with sudden drama, demanding in the loud tones of the hard of hearing to be taken to the bride. Mrs Morgan detached herself from a group of friends and rushed over to the old lady in concern.

'Aunt Clarice! Wherever have you been?'

In a welter of explanations and adjustments to her hearing aid, Miss Clarice Morgan eventually made it clear that the neighbour who was to have brought her had been taken ill, and his grandson had kindly stepped into the breach and driven her from Abergavenny.

'You should have asked someone to telephone, Auntie,' said Mrs Morgan reproachfully.

'No time for all that,' snapped the old woman, then turned to beckon imperiously to the young man hovering diffidently in the foyer. 'Come *along*, Christopher, stop dawdling out there.'

Reluctantly the tall, fair boy came to receive the thanks of the Rector and his wife, demurring when pressed to join them at the wedding breakfast, with the excuse of not being suitably dressed, but capitulating suddenly when Mari-Sîan strolled over casually and added her persuasion.

Sarah watched with amusement as Mari-Sîan netted her catch with an ease that smacked of long practice, and turned back to Rhodri to find he'd been annexed by friends who were obviously agog with curiosity to see him in such close attendance on Sarah. It was all the opportunity Rupert needed. Instantly he was beside her, blocking her instinctive move to escape.

'Come out into the foyer for a moment, Sarah,' he ordered, a look on his face she knew of old.

'No,' she said defiantly, and stood her ground.

'Sarah.' His voice dropped as he leaned closer and spoke almost directly into her ear, his breath hot on her lobe, making her jaw tighten. 'If you don't come voluntarily I shall pick you up and carry you out in full view of all your sister's guests.'

She turned freezing blue eyes on his set face. 'You wouldn't——' then she stopped. It was quite obvious he would. 'You bastard,' she said quietly, and gave him a meaningless, social smile. 'Two minutes. Not a second more.'

Rupert inclined his head, and with an abortive look at Rhodri's back which was momentarily turned, Sarah accompanied Rupert from the room, smiling politely at the various faces turned in greeting as they passed. Once through the doors Rupert caught her wrist in iron fingers and marched her outside, where they both stood staring at the beautiful tree-fringed greens of the golf course in simmering silence before he burst out. 'Why the hell didn't you stay and let me explain yesterday?'

Sarah looked at him with incredulous distaste. 'I would have thought that was glaringly obvious!'

'There was a perfectly simple explanation for what you saw——'

'Yes, I know.' Sarah smiled at him in pitying fashion that plainly set his strong white teeth on edge. 'Though I would have said basic, rather than simple. There's really nothing more to say.'

'If you will just listen for a moment, Sarah——'

'No. Nothing you can say can be of the slightest interest to me.' Sarah turned on her fragile heel with disdain, only to be jerked violently back to face Rupert once more.

'It was not in the least as you imagined, Sarah,' he said roughly, the colour rising along his cheekbones. 'Naomi——'

Sarah shied at the name like a half-broken thoroughbred. 'Take your hand away. I want to go back.'

Rupert's grip tightened, heavy as a manacle, his green eyes dark with rage. 'By God I'll make you listen somehow!'

Still holding her with one hand he began to search in the breast-pocket of his Calvin Klein waistcoat. Sarah stared, unbelieving, as he produced the turquoise and diamond ring and drew the thin doeskin glove from her left hand. At the sight of the five great sapphires glittering on the ring finger he dropped her other hand abruptly. For seconds they remained in tableau, then Rupert straightened, his nostrils dented white, and pushed the turquoise ring back in his pocket with fingers unsteady with rage. He smiled at Sarah's frozen face with a sneering twist of his mouth, his eyes empty of expression.

'It seems explanations are necessary on both sides,' he murmured, then gave a mocking little bow. 'Do forgive me. I've kept you out here much too long. It's time I returned you to the donor of that rather flamboyant little trifle you're sporting.'

'But——' Sarah came to life abruptly, as Rupert held up a graceful, admonitory hand.

'But me no buts, Sarah. My apologies for behaving in such oafish, though misguided fashion. If it were possible I'd take my leave right now, but your family hardly merit such a display of inexcusable manners on what should be a very happy day for them. Let's go in.'

Her heart like lead Sarah obeyed him automatically, walking in silence at Rupert's side as they returned to the festive hubbub of the reception. He left her immediately, with the briefest of nods, and went off to join Mari-Sîan and the group of young relatives with her. Sarah watched him go, then turned at a touch on her arm, to find Rhodri's grey eyes studying her intently.

'Trouble, Sarah?' He jerked his head in Rupert's direction. 'Your celebrity is causing quite a ripple in the pond. Is he being difficult?'

Sarah pulled herself together. 'Rupert Clare is invariably difficult, Rhodri—just more sometimes than others, I suppose.' She smiled philosophically. 'Father's beckoning, I think it's time we did something about eating.'

The meal was a blur afterwards in Sarah's mind. She cut up and pushed around the food on her plate, quite unable to eat any of it, though she gratefully accepted the champagne offered her, hoping it would help her to feel more festive. It failed miserably, but she smiled and laughed with the rest at the witty bits of the speeches, comforted by the presence of Rhodri at her side, attractive in his light Italian suit and the apparent affectation of the dark glasses, his smile in readiness even when a gushing, envious cousin asked if he and Sarah had chosen their clothes to match each other. Extra sensory perception, he informed her, his look at Sarah so proprietary it made her all the more conscious of Rupert's glittering smile wreaking havoc on the women in his vicinity on the other side of the room. She cursed him silently, smiling back at Rhodri with a warmth that brought a questioning twist to his mouth, and caused Rupert to turn his back abruptly in satisfying reaction.

When Sarah helped Rhia change later in the room hired for the purpose, the new Lady Hadley cast a questioning look at her. 'You look shattered, Sarah. Anything wrong?'

Sarah shook her head and zipped up the back of Rhia's apricot linen dress, then handed her the featherlight cashmere coat that went with it. 'I'm fine. I got up too early, that's all.'

Mari-Sîan was sitting watching them, her eyes sharp on Sarah's pale face. 'Are you sure there was no difference of opinion when you and your divine boss disappeared outside together?' she asked slyly. 'Was there a punch-up?'

'No, of course not.' Sarah smiled carelessly. 'Just a little consultation on his book and so on. Nothing personal.' She crossed mental fingers, wishing Mari-Sîan's myopic eyes had less perception.

Rhia smiled at Sarah and picked up her bag. 'You really are lucky, darling. Most girls would give their eye-teeth to work for a man like that.'

'The novelty soon wears off, I assure you.' Sarah glanced at her watch, frowning. 'What do you suppose Mother is doing? I thought she was supposed to be in here, drenching you with tears at the thought of losing a daughter.'

'Aunt Clarice buttonholed her as she was trying to get away.' Mari-Sîan grinned widely at Sarah. 'Apparently she'd got wind of the news about you and Rhodri. When I passed by she had her hearing-aid turned up, firing questions at Mam like the head of the KGB.'

Sarah groaned. 'I've managed to keep out of her range so far. I thought it was too good to be true.'

'Never mind,' soothed Rhia. 'That nice boy is taking her back soon—unless our junior femme-fatale here has prevailed otherwise.'

'No way.' Mari-Sîan wrinkled her nose scornfully. 'Compared to the hunky, divine Rupert Clare he just shrivelled into insipidity. Quite sweet, but, alas, square and boring.'

The door opened and Elizabeth Morgan hurried in breathlessly.

'Rhia, darling, I'm so sorry! Aunt Clarice heard about Sarah and Rhodri and had me penned up against that bank of flowers wanting to know every last thing about it, not to mention a complete run-down on Charles, from his income to whether you intend to start a family straight away.'

'If she weren't Father's aunt I'd tell her to get——' Rhia cut off the rest and gave her mother a hug. 'Don't worry, Sarah helped me out of my dress.'

'You look just as lovely in that one,' said Mrs Morgan, her eyes wet. 'And now you're Lady Hadley—it seems like only the other day. . . .'

'Oh come on, Mam!' Mari-Sîan patted her mother's shoulder. 'In a minute you'll be talking about your fledgelings flying the nest and all that sort of drivel.'

'Hardly,' Mrs Morgan replied with dignity. 'Rhia and Sarah left the nest a long time ago—and you'll be off too in a little while.'

'Don't tempt Providence,' warned her youngest child, touching wood. 'Anyway, let's just get her ladyship here off for the time being. We can worry over me later.'

After Rhia and Charles drove off in a welter of confetti and good wishes, bound for a luxury journey aboard the Orient Express for a brief stay in Venice before going on a cruise, the guests were left to disperse with the inevitable feeling of anticlimax that follows the departure of the bride and groom. To Sarah's horror she could hear her father asking Rupert back to the Rectory later that evening to join the small group of family and friends invited to supper.

'Go on,' urged Mari-Sîan, clutching Sarah's arm. 'Persuade him to come, Sal. He'll add a bit of excitement to the Morgan soirée—he's such fun, apart from being a celebrity.'

'Fun' was about the last description Sarah would have used to describe an evening spent with Rupert Clare and Rhodri Lloyd-Ellis within spitting distance of each other. Putting on an act as Rhodri's fiancée for the benefit of other people the entire day was wearing enough without Rupert as a member of the audience.

'I hardly think so,' she said flatly. 'Much too rustic. Not the sort of thing he's used to.' With a sinking feeling Sarah saw her father's long, narrow hand beckoning her, and with Mari-Sîan close behind her she joined her parents and Rupert, the latter in process of taking his leave.

'Add your persuasion to ours,' her father said, putting an arm round Sarah fondly. 'We're trying to cajole Mr Clare into staying on for our little party this evening.'

'We'd be very pleased—honoured, in fact,' added Mrs Morgan eagerly.

Rupert smiled at Sarah, the glint in his eyes letting her know he was very much aware of the tumult raging beneath her deceptively calm exterior. 'That's extraordinarily kind of you.' His eyes held Sarah's deliberately for a second longer before returning to her parents. 'Unfortunately I have a prior engagement, otherwise I would have been only too delighted to accept.'

There was a chorus of sincere regrets from all the Morgans except Sarah, who kept conspicuously quiet as she watched Rupert pulling out all the stops as he made his farewells. She began to relax just a little when it actually seemed Rupert might be on the point of leaving, then stiffened again as she realised what he was saying.

'Before I leave I need a brief word with Sarah, just boring shop I'm afraid, then I really must be on my way.' Elegant and self-assured in his superbly tailored suit, Rupert turned to Sarah with a casual smile. 'Just a moment of your time, Sarah, if you would.' He took her arm, his fingers tightening cruelly through the silk as he felt her recoil, then smiled at the others. 'Goodbye again. It's been a great pleasure to meet Sarah's family.'

Hiding her impatience with the expressions worn *en masse* by the others, Sarah had no option but to allow Rupert to lead her away towards the car park. She bore stoically with the fingers biting into her arm, deeply conscious of a great many pairs of interested eyes trained on their backs. Once they reached the conspicuous white Rolls Corniche Rupert released her and leaned indolently against the bonnet, his eyes hard.

'Thank you,' she said bitterly, and resisted the impulse

to rub her throbbing arm. 'You were endangering my circulation.'

'It's not your circulation that's in danger,' he said tightly. 'When are you coming back to St John's Wood?'

Sarah regarded him dispassionately. 'Unlike you to be obtuse, Rupert—you don't seem to be getting the message. I'm not *coming* back.' She felt a deep satisfaction as she watched him exert savage self-control on his emotions.

'You mean you actually intend to allow one misleading, easily explained incident to spoil our whole lives?' There was a pulse throbbing at the corner of Rupert's tightly compressed mouth; a bad sign, as Sarah knew from experience.

'I think it's more a matter of *not* spoiling the rest of our lives. We're both leopards with spots neither of us can, or will change.' Sarah lifted her head to meet his stormy eyes. 'I hope I'm not such a moron as to expect perfection. The thing is, Rupert, you could commit any number of sins of varying degree that wouldn't affect our relationship in the slightest. The one you chose, unfortunately, was the exception—no.' She held up a peremptory hand as Rupert began to speak. 'Hear me out. It's best we discovered our incompatibility at this stage, rather than later. I'm sure it won't come as too much of a surprise to you to learn that, with my background, I'm archaic enough to believe in the sanctity of marriage.'

At this Rupert's face lost some of its colour and his attitude its indolence. He straightened to his full height and looked down into Sarah's face with a bleak look that was unfamiliar and chilling.

'That would seem to be that, then,' he said in an off-hand, rather bored way that made Sarah's hackles rise. 'The prisoner stands down from the dock.' He turned away and got in the car, giving her a musing look. 'I would have bet my last penny that you possessed that rarest of female qualities—a sense of justice, Sarah. How very irritating to be proved wrong.' Rupert gave her the facile, meaningless smile she hated and set the car in motion, leaving her to watch numbly as it glided silently away. For a moment Sarah remained where she was, conscious of a searing sense of loss, and with the cheerless conviction that her last boat had just been burned behind her. She straightened her shoulders, summoning back her previous indignation to comfort her, wondering just how Rupert had succeeded in leaving her feeling that any transgressions concerned were hers. Then she walked back to Rhodri's comforting presence, glad her father was ignorant of the mental epithets she was hurling at her erstwhile employer. Sarah's footsteps faltered momentarily as she remembered that as yet her family had no idea just how erstwhile he was.

CHAPTER FIVE

By the time the Morgans' family party was over later that night Sarah felt limp with fatigue.

'I had no idea deception was such an exhausting business.' She smiled ruefully at Rhodri in the mellow glow from the old Victorian street lamp in the rectory garden. The last of the guests had finally departed, and although it was almost midnight the air was warm and very still under an indigo sky spattered with stars. Rhodri leaned against the Porsche, legs crossed and arms folded, his eyes steady on Sarah's face in the soft light.

'Only white lies, Sarah.' He straightened and took her hand. 'Perhaps we could get together some time tomorrow and have a talk—a plan of campaign.'

'Yes, of course,' she agreed instantly. 'I'll do my very best to get you off the hook as soon as humanly possible——'

'That's not quite what I meant,' he said swiftly. 'The hook in question was entirely my own idea, remember.'

'Even so I still feel guilty.' Sarah's face was troubled as she stared down at their joined hands. 'I'm deeply indebted to you, Rhodri.'

She tensed as his arm slid round her waist and drew her gently towards him until they were just touching.

'Then would it be in order if I collected just one chaste kiss on account?' he asked softly.

Sarah nodded silently, yielding him her mouth for a kiss that, to her dismay, proved to be anything but chaste on Rhodri's part.

'I'm sorry,' he said unevenly as he released her. 'That was underhand. You could hardly refuse, and somehow the kiss was a lot less chaste than I intended.'

'Yes it was.' Sarah stepped away, and gave him a wary little smile. 'Let's consider it as a token of appreciation.'

'Are you free tomorrow afternoon?' he asked diffidently. 'If I promise to keep my distance, that is.'

Sarah laughed. 'Yes, of course. Late-ish, though. Gareth and his harem leave after lunch, so perhaps we could go for a walk afterwards, as long as I'm back in good time for Evensong.'

'About three, then. Goodnight, Sarah, sleep well.'

'Goodnight, Rhodri—and thank you for all your help.'

Contrary to the restless night she anticipated Sarah slept as soon as her head touched the pillow, and stayed fast asleep all night until the early birdsong outside woke her to sunlight and total recall of her various problems. Sarah was profoundly grateful to have been granted a good night's rest, at least, feeling that her misery over Rupert was more than enough, without adding exhaustion to her list of troubles. She crept downstairs, dressed in the black skirt and blouse, her white jacket over her shoulders, and slipped out of the house before the rest of the family was awake, making her way through the garden and the orchard to the churchyard to gladden her father's heart by her presence in the old church at early communion. She offered up a silent plea to be granted both a state of grace and deliverance from her heartache, then accompanied her father home for breakfast. Sarah sat down to the crisp curls of bacon and glossy scrambled eggs rapidly produced by her mother, without the heart to refuse the food, but with very little appetite.

'How long will you stay, cariad?' Glyn Morgan asked quietly, aware of her lack of enthusiasm.

Sarah put down her knife and fork. 'I'm not really sure, Dad; a week or so perhaps—if that's all right?'

The expression on both her parents' faces was answer enough, and it seemed best to defer her news about giving up her job until a later date, when she had grown a little more accustomed to the idea herself.

Rhodri appeared punctually at three, long before Gareth and Jane had rounded up the four children and the dog and packed the car with the mountain of luggage apparently necessary for their brief stay. After much badinage and affectionate farewells Gareth's carload eventually left for home and Sarah and Rhodri set out for their walk, taking the footpath that began near the lych gate of the churchyard and continued steeply upwards through the woods behind it to wind over the rounded green hills beyond.

They climbed in companionable silence for a while, the narrowness of the path making it necessary to walk in single file. Rhodri went ahead to shield Sarah from encroaching branches of the close-clustering bushes and trees along the overgrown path, and she was hard put to keep up with his long, rapid stride, calling a halt as soon as they emerged on the open ground higher up. After an interval to allow her to catch her breath Rhodri took Sarah by the waist and lifted her over the stile, vaulting over to take her hand as they started up the gentle slope of the first rise, deserted on this hot, sunlit afternoon. They reached the brow and paused to look at a view familiar to both of them from childhood, an undulating vista of wooded slopes and tree-shadowed valleys whose solitude and peace were a far cry from the pace of the city that was the usual habitat of them both.

By mutual consent they both sank down on the velvety sheep-cropped turf, Sarah sitting cross-legged in her red linen trousers and the white tennis shirt and grubby plimsolls borrowed from Mari-Sîan. It was very still, the drone of bees loud among the clover, and Rhodri lay on his side, propped up on one elbow, a stalk of grass between his teeth as he watched Sarah making a rather inexpert daisy-chain, the concealing dark lenses successfully keeping any hint of what he was thinking from Sarah.

'What do we do now, Rhodri?' she asked abruptly, and abandoned her daisies.

He shrugged. 'Nothing.'

'What do you mean, nothing? We should be thinking of some way to get you out of this ridiculous charade for a start!' She frowned at him impatiently.

'What's so ridiculous about our being engaged?' His brows rose above the sunglasses in query.

Frustrated, Sarah sighed, running a rather sweaty hand through her hair. 'From my point of view nothing at all. The difficult member of the Rector's family and the heir to Cwmderwen Court—what more could I ask? The stuff fantasies are made of. Nevertheless all the advantages of the situation are mine——'

'Oh I wouldn't say that,' he murmured, and edged a little closer. 'There are compensations I could think of.' A faint smile played round his mouth.

Sarah eyed him with suspicion. 'If you mean physical compensation——'

'Of course I do.' His answer was so prompt Sarah stiffened, glaring at him.

'Then you can forget it. Here's your rotten ring and I'll go home and tell——'

'For God's sake, Sarah!' Rhodri's hand shot out and closed over hers cruelly. He glared back, his anger clearly visible, dark glasses notwithstanding. 'What's up with you, woman——'

She pulled away fiercely. 'Not you as well!'

'Now what's bitten you?'

'I loathe being called "woman" as though it were some form of insult,' said Sarah bitterly, 'and I'm not about to have sex with you as some form of compensation for your services either.'

Rhodri stared at her in distaste, his expression chilling as her words hit him like missiles.

'I was alluding to our goodnight kiss, Sarah.' His voice took on an austere note that transformed him instantly into a remote stranger. 'What kind of animal do you think I am? Are you expecting me to leap on you here in broad sunlight in full view of anyone who might pass by? For one thing I gave up rolling around in fields with girls in my teens. And as regards thanks or payment, I don't want any at all, verbal, physical or any other way.' He rose to his feet in one graceful movement and held out a perfunctory hand to help Sarah up. She looked up at him uncertainly, ashamed of her hasty conclusions, and unsure how to make reparation.

'I'm sorry, Rhodri, I'm a pig. Particularly when you've been so——'

'Forget it.' He flung away from her and stood staring into the distance, hands in pockets. Sarah moved nearer and put a hand on his arm.

'Could we kiss and make up?' she ventured, smiling crookedly at his wary reaction. He frowned down at her, his eyes narrowed as she went on, 'Only you'll have to unbend, mentally and physically. I can't reach you.'

Rhodri smiled, to her relief, and took off his sunglasses.

'Try harder,' he said softly, and bent his head to receive Sarah's kiss of apology as she stood on tiptoe. The touch of Rhodri's firm mouth was pleasant, so was the feel of his strong arms holding her, but, like the night before, Sarah felt no leap of response inside her, no quickening of the pulse or difficulty in breathing. It was just another kiss, like all the other kisses experienced before she came up against Rupert and the electrifying effect of even the slightest touch of his hand. Gently she disengaged herself, giving a fleeting look at Rhodri as he fell into step beside her, looking away before he could meet her eyes. Grateful for his companionable silence Sarah felt an odd sense of disappointment. How strange life was. A few short years ago a kiss from Rhodri Lloyd-Ellis would have fulfilled all her wildest dreams, yet now it meant nothing after the intensity of Rupert's lovemaking. Rhodri was one of the nicest men she had ever met, thought Sarah despairingly, so why wasn't it possible to fall in love with *him*, instead of a philandering brute like Rupert?

'You look hot—am I going too fast for you?' Rhodri was looking at her flushed face in concern.

'No, of course not. I have to be back shortly anyway, to get ready for Evensong. My second visit to church today, I might add!'

He grinned. 'The perfect Rector's daughter.'

Sarah's smile faded as she shook her head. 'The Rector may be perfect, his daughter most certainly is not.'

Rhodri leaned beside her, taking his glasses off to look

at her, a frown creasing his tanned forehead. 'In what way are you so imperfect, Sarah?'

'Well, this morning I made my first visit to church since I left home at eighteen, for a start.' She turned to gaze into the shade of the trees lining the footpath down to the church. 'Do you know, Rhodri, that Father not only had the delicacy and forbearance never to ask that I went to church during my infrequent visits home, but this morning there was no production about it when I finally did put in an appearance at communion either. I felt somewhat small.'

Rhodri slid an arm around her waist and gave her a squeeze, grinning. 'Well, you *are* small.'

'It's unlikely I'll grow any more physically, but boy is there room for improvement where my character's concerned.' Sarah sighed and chewed her lip as she leaned against him, unconsciously finding comfort in his proximity. 'I may sound prosy, but I think life is punctuated with crossroads at intervals. I came to the first when the crash altered everything, and now I feel that this weekend has been another landmark, a difference in direction.'

Rhodri turned her to face him, looking down at her with something in his clear grey eyes that troubled her a little.

'Away from Rupert Clare?' he asked gently.

Sarah turned away, unwilling to answer. 'I don't know. I suppose so—in fact I haven't the remotest idea what I'll do with myself for the moment,' she said. 'I've told the parents I'm home on holiday for a bit. I'll get out and around with Mari-Sîan, if she's agreeable, go for walks, or even just lie in the sun if this weather continues. I've been working at full pressure lately, so I'll be glad of a break.'

Rhodri lifted her over the stile and they went down the narrow, overhung path, passing through the lychgate into the churchyard, pausing a moment at the gate into the rectory orchard.

'Will you have a meal with me tonight, Sarah?' he asked, not attempting to take her hand this time.

Sarah shook her head apologetically. 'I don't think so, Rhodri.' She met his eyes squarely. 'You've been marvellous over this weekend. I'm grateful—very grateful. But tonight I think I ought to be at home with the family.'

Rhodri opened the gate, ushering her through with a slight withdrawal in his manner that Sarah registered with dismay.

'Are you offended?' she asked.

'No, of course not.' He shrugged ruefully. 'I'm not the most tactful of people, am I? Naturally you want some time to yourself, I'll call round in a day or two, shall I?'

'Of course. I'll take good care of the ring.'

'Hang on to it for the time being.' Rhodri gave her a playful little punch on the chin and sauntered off through the garden, waving as he turned through the gate.

A quiet evening with the family was something of an anticlimax, but after the family's return from church it was a very welcome respite for Sarah from the drama of the past couple of days. Mrs Morgan was looking distinctly weary, and for once allowed her daughters to bully her into sitting quietly with their father while they concocted a cold supper from the abundant supply of left-overs from the night before, and the rest of the evening was so tranquil Sarah had no heart to upset her parents with the news that she was jobless, and with no adequate reason to give for leaving such a good post so abruptly. The truth would have been as unpalatable to them as it was to herself, and she had no stomach for any further fabrications, so she kept quiet.

Next morning Mari-Sîan returned to school for the final few days before leaving it for good, and after helping to put the house to rights Sarah was enjoying a mid-morning cup of coffee with her parents when the doorbell rang. The Rector got to his feet with a sigh, draining his coffee cup hastily.

'I'll have another when I get back, Beth. Don't drink the pot dry.'

His wife looked after him, frowning. 'I had hoped for a

quiet day today. Glyn's always a little tired on Mondays, but this weekend has been a lot for him.' She met Sarah's eyes, her own troubled. 'I haven't mentioned it to the others, love, but your father's heart isn't as strong as it might be. Mild angina, the doctor says, and if he takes care he can go on for years, but I must try to shield him from shocks and anxiety. As if I haven't done that all our married life——' she broke off guiltily as her husband came back into the room. 'That was quick, Glyn, who was it?'

'A visitor for Sarah. Mr Clare—I've put him in the drawing room. You'd better make more coffee, Beth.' His eyes narrowed as he noticed his daughter's sudden pallor.

Mrs Morgan stared at her husband before springing up to refill the percolator, looking questioningly at Sarah, who was momentarily struck dumb.

'Did you know he was coming this morning, Sarah?'

Sarah took a deep breath. 'No. I didn't.'

'Change your shirt and jeans quickly, love.' Her mother gave a disparaging look at the faded garments in question as she swiftly set a tray with her best coffee-cups. Sarah pulled herself together.

'Why?' she said carelessly. 'I'm on holiday.'

She left the kitchen unhurriedly and paused a moment in the hall, well aware of the speculation she left behind her. Gritting her teeth she opened the door of the room she had diligently polished and vaccuumed earlier, and head up, went in to confront her unwelcome visitor.

Rupert Clare stood at the window, looking out on the garden at the back of the house, the scent of the honeysuckle cascading over the dry-stone wall strong in the cool room. In pale grey linen trousers with a sleeveless grey cashmere pullover and white shirt, Rupert looked elegant in an understated way, putting Sarah at an immediate disadvantage as he swung round to take in her dishevelled appearance with a cool smile. She felt hot and grubby, and consequently even less well-disposed towards him than before.

'Why are you here?' she asked without preamble.

'Good morning, Sarah.' Rupert shook his head reprovingly. 'Tut, tut, what manners! Certainly not inherited from your father; a man of infinite charm from my brief acquaintance with him.'

'As you say,' she replied tonelessly. They faced each other in the middle of the room like two pugilists sizing each other up in a boxing ring, Sarah hot with resentment as she stared up at him. 'I wouldn't have put you down as lacking in perception, Rupert, even less as possessing diminished aural powers, but perhaps you just weren't paying attention when I said I never wanted to see or hear from you again.'

'Such melodrama!' Rupert waved her to a chair politely. 'Sit down, Sarah, and let us have a quiet, sensible talk.'

Sarah was prevented from exploding only by the entry of her mother with the coffee-tray, which Rupert sprang to take from her.

'Good morning, Mrs Morgan, delightful to see you again.' His smile had a potent effect on Sarah's mother, and she beamed in return.

'How nice of you to drop in, Mr Clare, I didn't realise you were staying on in the area. Yes, on that table. Thank you.'

Rupert sent a look of delicate reproach at Sarah's still, watchful face as he set down the tray. 'My next book is to be set partly in Monmouth at the time of Henry the Fifth. Did you not mention it, Sarah?'

'No.' As it was news to Sarah it was hardly surprising. 'It must have slipped my mind.'

Mrs Morgan smiled apologetically. 'We've been so taken up with the wedding, then with Sarah's happy news as well, it's small wonder she forgot. Sarah, I'll leave you to serve coffee, I'm sure you both have a lot to discuss.'

As the door closed behind Mrs Morgan Rupert sauntered over to the sofa and sat down, relaxed and indolent as Sarah unwillingly handed him a cup of the black, sweet coffee he liked.

'Thank you, Sarah.' His mouth curved in a smile that stopped short of his cold green eyes. 'Your mother is more accurate than she knows. We have a great deal to discuss, don't you agree?'

With resignation Sarah sat down to listen to whatever Rupert had come to say. 'Very well,' she said briskly, 'several topics occur to me. Which would you like?' She sat back in her chair, hands folded in her lap her eyes fixed on Rupert's face with polite attention. Rupert finished his coffee without hurry, then leaned back, crossing his legs, a look of enquiry in his eyes.

'Presumably your parents don't know that you no longer intend working with me?' he asked carefully.

Sarah nodded. 'I haven't broken it to them yet.'

'You use the word "broken"—does that mean the news will be unwelcome?'

'Yes. Loss of a job is hardly ever a matter for celebration.'

Rupert looked around him at the charming, but rather shabby room. There were several good pieces of furniture, the wood glossy with the patina of constant care, but the brocade on the sofa and chairs was worn, and the curtains and carpet had obviously been in service for a long time. He placed his hands together, making a steeple of his fingers and avoided the chill blue eyes of the girl who sat very still as she watched him.

'I don't wish to give offence, Sarah——'

'How surprising—since you do it with such consummate ease!' She turned her head to stare through the open window, and Rupert's jaw tightened as he went on quietly.

'Neither have I any wish to pry into your family's private concerns, but I can't help feeling your lack of salary will be a blow to them. I haven't a clue what sort of stipend a clergyman receives, but Mari-Sîan was telling me on Saturday that she hopes to go up to Oxford next term, and there was Rhia's wedding to finance.' He looked up in time to catch an arrested expression on Sarah's face as her anger was replaced by anxiety.

'What exactly are you getting at Rupert?' she asked, all her attention apparently centred on the garden outside. He got up and went over to crouch by her chair, putting out a finger to turn her face to his.

'Very well. Let's get things straight.' There was nothing intimate or personal in his manner, and he dropped his hand the moment Sarah faced him, his eyes hooded and unreadable. 'I don't know exactly how you managed to produce another fiancé in such double-quick time—by my calculations somewhere in the region of eight hours—therefore I assume you met Lloyd-Ellis somewhere on the way home, and being an old chum he chivalrously agreed to stand in as surrogate suitor in a sort of face-saving mission.'

Sarah kept still with an effort, his nearness trying her sorely.

'Full marks for deduction, Rupert, you should be writing crime novels,' she said lightly, 'but you chose the wrong word. For "agreed" substitute "volunteered". I met Rhodri on the train purely by chance. He's an old friend of my brother's, but I hadn't met him since I left home. He—well, he could see I was somewhat upset, and suggested I confide in him, as we were just acquaintances and not likely to encounter each other again for years, probably.' Sarah gave him a faint, austere smile. 'Things didn't work out quite like that, though, in the end.'

Rupert rose to his feet with a jerk, and moved over to the window, his back to her. 'How precisely did you persuade him to—stand in for me?' His voice rasped in its effort to remain dispassionate.

'It wasn't like that. Come on, Rupert, be realistic! I'm the Rector's daughter and he's the son and heir of the local landowner, not to mention grandson of an earl. The thought of asking him, or anyone else, to do something so crazy would never have entered my mind.'

'It entered his easily enough,' he said coldly, turning round.

'He was sorry for me. I had told my mother the night before that my mystery guest was my—my future husband, God help me, idiotically insisting on keeping your identity as a surprise, complete with triumphant arrival in your Rolls.' Sarah's voice was bitter with self-loathing. 'I left home originally under something of a cloud, and I was childish enough to want to return with flags flying. When I did arrive the entire family streamed out of the house to see me getting out of a car with Rhodri Lloyd-Ellis. Before I could say a word he jumped in at the deep end and told them *he* was my surprise.' She stopped, gripping her hands tightly together to stop them trembling.

'And what car did *he* have?' asked Rupert unexpectedly, a sneer in his voice.

Sarah stiffened. 'A Porsche. What difference does it make?'

He shrugged. 'You seem to attach great importance to the manner of your arrival. Perhaps I can be forgiven for wondering if the eligibility of your escort, and the quality of his possessions are the factors that weigh most with you—more than the actual man. Were you shattered by what you thought you saw in my room for entirely the right reasons, Sarah?'

Sarah was assailed by an overwhelming urge to assault him with one of her mother's treasured Meissen figurines. She glared at him in outrage.

'Are you insinuating that I agreed to marry you just because you're wealthy and famous?' Even as the words left her mouth she regretted them.

'It had crossed my mind.' Rupert strolled across the room, his swagger much in evidence. 'If I were still an impecunious reporter living in a shabby bedsitter would my proposal have been accepted quite as promptly, I wonder?'

Sarah rolled down the sleeves of her tatty gingham shirt, suddenly cold. 'If that's what you wish to believe I shan't exert myself to persuade you otherwise,' she said dully.

Rupert watched her, head on one side, a hatefully reasonable look on his face. 'At first glance that's how it seems, Sarah. And you're the one who lays great store in taking everything at face value, with no qualifying explanations accepted.'

Sarah felt defeated. She glanced wearily at the mocking comprehension on Rupert's face, knowing that nothing on earth would drag out of her the admission that who he was or what he possessed had never meant anything beside the wonder of the feelings he evoked in her. She had wanted the man for himself, and himself alone, from the moment she first saw him.

'Explain then,' she said coldly. 'I can't for the life of me see what possible explanation there could be for what I saw, apart from the obvious one.'

'Then I shan't exert myself to explain either,' Rupert answered indifferently. Suddenly he was brisk. 'We've wandered from the point. To return to the subject of finances; presumably your family would have no anxiety about your lack of job if they thought you were on the point of marrying Lloyd-Ellis.'

'As you know better than anyone that I am not, nor am I marrying you, nor anyone else. Which still doesn't alter my feelings on the subject of working for you.' Sarah's chin lifted resolutely. 'I'll get another job in London——'

'Not so easy nowadays,' he reminded her.

'I can live on my savings while I'm looking,' she said loftily, then stopped, a sudden recollection bringing her up short. In an uncharacteristic fit of extravagance she had spent a small fortune on clothes to show off in over the past weekend, plus the expensive silver rose-bowl given to Rhia as a wedding present. Her small flat was modest, but nevertheless costly, and without a regular salary cheque coming in, even for a short while, the outlook was bleak.

Rupert read her mind with infuriating ease. He took her cold, unresisting hand and led her to the sofa. Sarah sat limply, hardly noticing when he sat down close beside her, his body half-turned towards her.

'Now listen to me, Sarah, and don't interrupt.'

At the note of command in his voice she opened her mouth instinctively to protest, then shut it again as he motioned her sharply to silence.

'I intend staying in Monmouth for the next few days,' he began, his manner deliberately business-like. 'My next opus is centred round a fictitious nobleman, meant to be one of the "happy few" who fought at Agincourt with Harry of Monmouth. The king himself is to feature in the book so I thought I'd start here at his birthplace, then spend some time in France. I need a lot of information on contemporary warfare, weapons, dress, customs and so on, the type of details you research so very efficiently for me.'

'And the lady in the plot?' asked Sarah, interested against her will.

'A damsel of Yorkist sympathies, which nearly gets our hero executed for treason.' Rupert paused, holding her eyes. 'He almost swerves from his true allegiance because of his love for her.'

'It doesn't sound terribly true to the life of the time.' Sarah looked away. 'Expediency, not love, was the reason for attachments in those days. Marriage was a political or financial transaction, and men relieved the monotony of their legal obligations by having a "bit on the side"—or several.'

His eyebrows rose. 'Rather an unexpected phrase, coming from you Sarah!'

She smiled without amusement. 'Isn't a woman supposed to surprise a man now and then, to be interesting?'

'Stop diverting me, Sarah. What I'm asking is will you help me research, at least? You know I don't have half the patience for historical minutiae that you do. In the meantime I'll look for someone else to do the actual typing and eventually take over your job. A man this time,' he added heavily.

Sarah shook her head stubbornly. 'I won't come back to St John's Wood.'

'Very well.' Rupert's patience was obviously hanging

by a very thin thread. 'Work from home here, at least while I'm in Monmouth, then perhaps you could come to France for the other part, and I'll do the rest on my own.'

Sarah sat making rapid calculations in her head. The flat was paid up for the quarter and if she lived at home for a while there would be no housekeeping bills, as her mother would never recover from the hurt if Sarah offered payment for food. Whatever Rupert paid her could be added to the meagre remains in her savings account, her parents would be pleased if she remained at home for a while, and in the meantime she herself would be occupied with the research she loved so much. It would serve as a breathing space and give her the chance to scour the newspapers secretly for likely jobs against the day when she would have to resume the role of black sheep again, an unavoidable fate when it was learned that not only was she no longer working for her charismatic author, but neither was she likely to be the future chatelaine of Cwmderwen Court.

'Well?' he prompted.

Sarah stood up. 'All right. I'll do the research with you here, but that's all. No France and no St John's Wood. I shall be looking for other employment in the meantime.'

Rupert rose to his feet, his eyes sombre. The shadows beneath them seemed more pronounced than earlier, and something in his stance told her he was holding himself on a tight rein. The silence irked her.

'Was there anything else?' she asked politely.

'No. Can we make a start this afternoon? I'll call for you at two-thirty—if that's convenient?'

'Yes.'

Silence fell again, pulsating with words left unsaid. For what seemed like aeons Sarah's blue gaze remained locked with the brooding stare of the man who, for all he stood only an arm's length away, had put himself beyond her reach. Rupert moved a little nearer, the tension in his taut body communicating itself to hers as Sarah stood, wooden, her feet glued to the floor. The tip of her tongue flicked along her dry lips and the spell that held them was broken. His arms shot out and dragged her against him, his mouth crushing the protest on her before it was uttered. For a few, fleeting moments they kissed with an intensity and violence closer to hatred than desire, until the sound of footsteps in the hall outside drove them apart, Rupert swallowing hard and Sarah's cheeks flying red banners of guilt as Mrs Morgan came in to enquire if Mr Clare would stay to lunch. Rupert declined, to Sarah's heartfelt relief, and took graceful leave of her parents, who went with their daughter to the door to watch Rupert get in the big white car that took up almost all of the drive. Before he turned the key in the ignition Rupert looked at Sarah.

'Two-thirty then?'

She nodded, uneasily aware that she was asking for trouble, and that Rupert Clare was all too likely to be the donor, her eyes absently on the car as it glided silently out of sight. Over lunch her parents were deeply interested in the new novel, the Rector envious of Sarah's task in researching the subject, and providing many useful tips on sources and locations. They were delighted to hear that her stay was likely to be longer than they thought.

'You could have asked Mr Clare to stay here,' said Mrs Morgan.

'No thanks, Mam.' The old childhood name slipped out involuntarily. 'He can more than afford the expense, and you've had enough to cope with lately without catering for a stranger.'

Her mother subsided, half-relieved, half-disappointed. 'Ask him to a meal sometime then, Sarah.'

'I was favourably impressed by your author,' observed Glyn Morgan. 'None of the affectations I might have expected from someone who not only writes, but also seems to achieve quite extensive television coverage.'

'I didn't think you watched television much, Dad!' Sarah regarded her father with surprise.

'He's fond of those programmes where celebrities just sit about and talk to the host,' said Mrs Morgan, smiling.

'There was a clergyman *and* a historian on the first one he happened to see, and he was hooked—is that the right word?'

'Right on, Mam!' chuckled Sarah.

'Mr Clare came over very well on one programme taking on his early experiences as a reporter,' said her father. 'There was an actress, a very blonde lady, on the same programme who quite plainly found him tremendously absorbing.'

I'll bet she did, thought Sarah with acerbity, and refused dessert in favour of a speedy bath and shampoo and blow-dry for her hair, with the object of bolstering her morale for the afternoon with Rupert, unable to suppress the frisson of anticipation she felt all the time she was getting ready. When the doorbell rang promptly at two-thirty she was waiting, dressed in her red trousers and newly laundered white shirt, her white jacket over her shoulders as she opened the door to Rupert.

'Ready?' He ran an eye over her with undisguised appreciation. 'I like that. New?'

Sarah nodded, called out goodbye to her parents and followed Rupert outside, stopping in her tracks as she caught sight of the red Mini-Metro standing near the gate.

'Don't tell me!' he said dramatically. 'You've changed your mind now I no longer have the Rolls!'

'Where did that come from?' she demanded, laughing at the smug look on his face.

'I hired it, Miss Morgan. If we are to explore the surrounding countryside I felt a slightly smaller vehicle might be practical.' He held the door open for her with a flourish. Sarah got in, and looked round her appreciatively.

'It's sweet. Where's the Rolls?'

'In the hotel car park until I leave—have no fear, I still own it.'

Sarah shrugged, her momentary spark of friendliness dying at the sarcasm in Rupert's voice. 'Nothing to do with me.'

He scowled, then schooled his features to a neutral expression. 'Let's call a truce, Sarah, and enjoy the afternoon. The sun's shining and the land of your fathers looks like Eden. Let's sink our differences. Direct me on a magical mystery tour.'

'Suits me.' Sarah accepted the olive branch and smiled at him with something like her normal warmth, 'Sightseeing today, then, Rupert, but we get down to work in earnest tomorrow.'

'Done. So which way out of your gate, then, Sarah, or will you need a map?'

'Impertinence! No map for me, you ignorant Anglo-Saxon. Just turn left and prepare to wind your way into the past, via the labyrinthine byways of rural Gwent!'

Chuckling at Sarah's theatricality Rupert settled down to follow her directions, her description of their journey proving not nearly as fanciful as it sounded. They drove slowly along a meandering route that took in Skenfrith, one of the smallest of the thirteenth-century border castles, then on to White Castle on its hilltop, dating from the same time, then penetrating deep into the lovely valley of Ewyas to Llanthony where the ruins of the medieval Augustinian Priory stood bathed in tranquil sunshine in the lee of the Black Mountains.

Rupert stopped the car some distance away and sat looking in silence at the scene before him. Unconsciously his hand moved to close over Sarah's as she sat quietly beside him, letting him drink in his first view of the Priory. The scene was beloved and familiar to her, but she was well able to appreciate the effect on Rupert as he looked at it for the first time. After a while he reached over to the back seat of the car for his camera and got out of the car to record the scene on film, as he normally did when researching an area. Sarah stayed where she was, looking at his absorbed, clever face as he took several shots, her scrutiny unnoticed as she watched the grace of his slim, whipcord body moving from one side of the car to the other, his thick brown hair lifting in the slight, warm breeze of the summer afternoon. He turned and beckoned.

'Come out for a moment. Lean against the car and smile, Sarah,' he instructed. She got out reluctantly, looking at him in entreaty, with no wish to disturb their fragile amity, but hating the idea of a photograph of herself. Since her accident she had been morbidly camera-shy, and at the wedding had managed to elude all but two of the family photographs.

'I'm not in the least photogenic,' she said despairingly.

Rupert ignored her. 'Just lean casually against the bonnet—your colour-scheme blends with the paintwork. Come on, smile, woman, smile!'

'Rupert——'

He looked up from the view-finder, his eyes vividly green and direct in the bright light. He said quietly. 'If all I'm to have of you in future is one solitary photograph, Sarah, are you niggard enough to refuse me?'

Sarah had no answer, though the smile he demanded as she posed was a little unsteady and even more lopsided than usual as she gazed into the camera lens while he took not just one, but several shots of her.

'Behind all that medieval mysticism you may be glad to know there's a pub in the ruins,' she informed him as he put the camera away. Rupert grinned and looked at his watch.

'Not open yet—shall we go for a walk?'

'Oh I haven't finished with you yet! We go on up the valley to Capel-y-ffin. There's an Anglican Benedictine monastery there, founded by Father Ignatius in 1870.' Sarah slid into the car, aware that Rupert's eyes had narrowed to green slits as he joined her.

'Are you hoping that an odour of sanctity will adhere to me if you cart me around enough religious sites, darling? I warn you, I'm not really monastic material.'

Sarah laughed. 'Did I ask for miracles? I thought your noble hero might have sought shelter here at Llanthony, so it would be apposite, but if you want to skip the more modern establishment up the valley we can go back to Monmouth by a different route.'

'Let's find a nice, comfortable, grassy bank and lie in the sun for a while, then ply ourselves with foaming ale in yonder hostelry, after which I suggest we make for Monmouth, or any place you prefer, for a companionable dinner before I restore you to your family.' Rupert kept his eyes steadfastly on the ruins below them as he spoke, not using the powerful persuasion of his smile, and Sarah watched him curiously, noting that his hands were tight on the wheel. She could have sworn that her answer mattered to him more than his casual invitation suggested. She looked away hastily. If only there had been no painful early-morning revelation in Rupert's bedroom this could have been an idyllic journey of exploration, not only backward in time to the Monmouth of King Hal, but further forward in their discovery of each other.

'Well?' he asked huskily.

Sarah blinked. 'Yes,' she said briefly.

Rupert turned smiling eyes on her, shaking his head.

'On occasion you are a maddeningly monosyllabic creature, Sarah. Was that "yes" in answer to everything?'

'No. Just to the suggestions you made,' she assured him tartly, and got out of the car again, leaving him to follow her as she chose a suitable spot to enjoy the sun. They lounged together in silence for a while, Rupert apparently having no ready riposte to her last sally, content to lie beside her, his eyes fixed on the grey stones of the ruins.

'I rather thought you'd like it here,' said Sarah after a while. She hugged her arms round her drawn-up knees, noticing with a feeling of *déjà vu* that Rupert was propped up on one elbow in much the same attitude as Rhodri's the afternoon before, though minus the stalk of grass between his teeth.

'You always know instinctively,' he said quietly.

'Know what?'

'Exactly what will please me, Sarah.' Rupert's head was turned away. 'We've spent a lot of time together the past two or three years.'

'No,' she corrected swiftly. 'I've spent a lot of time in your house, Rupert, but you haven't always been there. It's only the past few months that your attention has turned to me, and sometimes I feel the only reason for that was because I represented a challenge.'

He moved restlessly, sitting upright, the sun glinting gold on the fine hairs on his forearms as he rested his weight on his hands.

'I always noticed you, Sarah. I wouldn't have asked you to work for me in the first place if you, well, if you hadn't appealed to me.'

'Rubbish! You needed someone there and then because you were in a hole. Anyone would have done who could have typed and wrestled with those tapes of yours.'

Rupert sighed, giving her a sidelong look intended to rouse her sympathy. 'And now you intend to abandon me.'

Sarah returned the look, unmoved. 'Yes, Rupert. Got it in one.'

He shrugged. 'It doesn't seem characteristic of you somehow, Sarah. You're over-reacting in my book.'

She pounced. 'Ah, but that's what life is all about to you, Rupert!' Her voice was biting as she got to her feet, looking down into his upturned face with scorn. 'It's all a story to you, and people are just characters in a plot. As far as I'm concerned, Mr Novelist, I intend to be the heroine in my story—*not* the other woman.'

Rupert sprang to his feet like a cat, and gripped her by the elbows, his eyes boring into hers. 'Why can't you believe me when I say that's exactly what you are, Sarah. There *are* no other women in my life in the way you mean.'

She shook her head blindly. 'How do you expect me to believe that?'

'Because it's God's truth, woman! Have you no trust in me at all?' There was a hoarse urgency in his voice that made Sarah's purpose waver, but only for an instant.

'I trust my own eyes, Rupert, and I know what I saw.'

He released her at once, impersonal once more. 'What you *think* you saw, darling. Quite different.'

Sarah stared at him uncertainly. 'Then tell me——' she began, but faltered into silence at the inexorable look on his face as he shook his head.

'No. I want you to take my word—to trust me, without any explanation. God, Sarah, am I asking so much?'

'Yes, you are! I'm only human, Rupert.'

'You surprise me, darling.' His smile cut her to pieces. 'Come on, let's see if this pub is open.'

Sarah shook her head blindly, swallowing a lump in her throat.

'No. I'd like to go home. Now, please.'

The convoluted route back hardly allowed for much speed, but they nevertheless returned to the rectory in less than half the time taken on their leisurely outward journey. Rupert swung the small car into the drive and brought it to an abrupt halt, the tyres crunching on the gravel as he turned to her, his face stony.

'Here you are, Sarah, home as you wanted. Goodbye.'

Sarah gave him an uncertain look, her full lower lip caught between her teeth.

'Well? What are you waiting for?' he demanded roughly.

'I was merely wondering if you were likely to want me tomorrow,' she said.

Rupert's mouth twisted. 'I want you now, right at this minute, Sarah. Don't blush—you're perfectly safe. I've no intention of ravishing you on your father's doorstep. No doubt I shall, in the fullness of time, stop wanting you, but for the time being I think you can safely assume that I do.'

'You know very well I was alluding to research.' Sarah got out of the car, tight-lipped.

Rupert leaned his head through the window. 'I'll be here at ten in the morning. Tell your parents you'll be out to lunch.' With an off-hand nod, he reversed the car neatly and drove off without a backward glance.

CHAPTER SIX

SARAH stood beneath the willows and watched him go, deflated as a pricked balloon. The truce had been shortlived. She felt disorientated and depressed, in no mood to go indoors to counter the inevitable questions from the family about her afternoon. On impulse she stole round the side of the house into the back garden and into the overgrown orchard beyond it. Her favourite retreat as a child had been up in the branches of one of the old apple trees, and after a moment's hesitation she managed to scramble up to her old perch, curling up out of sight among the branches. Somewhere near at hand woodpigeons were cooing, the peaceful sound gradually soothing Sarah's distress. Rupert was a great one to talk of 'wanting', she thought with bitterness; his heroes hardly ever used the word love to the objects of their affections. Lust, desire, these seemed to be the only feelings he understood. Her mouth drooped as she settled herself more comfortably against the trunk. If Rupert were freer with the verb to love, perhaps she might find it easier to trust. It was useless trying to delude herself that she no longer cared for him—the merest glimpse of him sent her mouth dry and her heart pounding. The sight of Naomi in Rupert's bed, all tumbled hair and naked shoulders, had been like a spear that pierced Sarah to the core. At the mere memory of Naomi and Rupert frozen in tableau in his bedroom that morning she felt physically sick again, but clamped down on the feeling sternly, searching back for any recollection of Rupert actually using the word love in his overtures to her.

Sarah sighed drearily. This was all fruitless now. Rupert, impossible as usual, required her unquestioning adoration and trust, without giving any reassurances in return, but there was no way she could yield herself up so completely. Rhodri would never be so unreasonable, she was sure. Rhodri. Sarah frowned. Something would have to be done about that too. She could hardly go on pulling the wool over her parents' eyes, but it would have to wait a little before she set things straight. And she would have to accomplish it with the least possible hurt and embarrassment to all concerned while she was at it. Sarah rubbed the small dent in her nose, sighing. She liked Rhodri very much. In fact she *liked* him a lot more than she liked Rupert. She disapproved strongly of some aspects of Rupert Clare, while Rhodri Lloyd-Ellis was the type of man who obviously played by the rules. She gave a little grunt of a laugh, doubting that Rupert was even aware there were any rules.

'Would you like yours brought out to you al fresco, or are you coming in to eat with the rest of us?' Mari-Sîan's voice interrupted her reverie loudly.

Sarah peered down through the branches at her sister's upturned face.

'I'll come down, of course—if I can!' Gingerly she felt for footholds, finding her descent a lot more difficult than the climb up. She landed with a thump on the grass beside Mari-Sîan, dusting off her expensive linen trousers with the palms of her hands. 'I'm out of practice.'

Mari-Sîan fell into step with her as they strolled slowly back to the house.

'We saw you sneaking round the back, and being the Soul of Tact, Mam thought we should leave you in peace until dinnertime.' She gave a bright, searching glance at Sarah. 'Trying afternoon, Sal?'

Sarah nodded briefly. 'A bit. Rupert's a bit exacting when he's getting the background of a new book.'

'I liked that one about the Renaissance *condottiere*, Giancarlo something—very sexy he was.' Mari-Sîan smacked her lips with relish. 'They kept it for me at the library.'

'If you've read any others you can't have failed to notice that all Rupert's male characters lean strongly to the chauvinistic,' said Sarah dryly.

'Self-portraits?'

'More than likely.'

'Rupert strikes me as being a lot randier than, say, Rhodri, for a start. Is he?'

Sarah gave her sister a push, laughing. 'Vulgar horror! Don't let Father hear you talking like that! Tell me, what are we eating?'

'That summer stew thing Mam does with lamb—come on, I'm starving.'

Sarah looked at her reflection with distaste next morning, and did her best to disguise the shadows under her tired eyes. Rupert's eagle eye would note signs of a sleepless night, she knew, so she applied more make-up than usual and dressed in her black blouse and skirt to look impersonal and efficient, then went down to join her parents for breakfast.

Her father looked up from his paper with a smile as her mother gave her a kiss and made enquiries as to her appetite.

'Toast, please,' said Sarah firmly. 'Nothing else—unless there's some of your own marmalade.'

'Where are you going today?' asked her father as Mrs Morgan quickly provided Sarah's request and sat down to pour tea.

'Monmouth itself today, to get some material on Henry himself—Rupert gets amazing stimulus just from looking at places and visualising his characters against authentic backgrounds. It's a pity there isn't more left of Monmouth castle, as it's Henry's birthplace, though Rupert was very taken with Skenfrith and White Castle yesterday.'

'I envy you, young lady. Yours is a very rewarding job, I imagine.' Glyn Morgan patted Sarah's head and handed her the daily paper as he departed for a round of sick visiting, leaving her feeling more guilty and depressed than ever. She had a quick look through the Situations Vacant in the *Daily Telegraph* while Mrs Morgan saw her husband off, but nothing looked in the least appealing, and Sarah's gloom deepened. She would be fortunate indeed to find another job anywhere near as lucrative or interesting as the one she was giving up.

'I've made another pot of tea.' Mrs Morgan sat down, pleased to have Sarah to herself. Head on one side she scanned her daughter's face before refilling their cups. 'You look a bit heavy-eyed this morning, love. Bad night?'

'A bit restless. I'm not used to a life of sloth like this.' Sarah smiled affectionately. 'Don't worry. After a day of running around after Rupert Clare, notebook at the ready, I'll be out for the count tonight.'

'You love your work darling?' Mrs Morgan's eyes were keen.

Sarah nodded absently, stirring her tea. 'Yes. I do. I'll be sorry to leave it.'

'You can hardly expect to carry on with it once you marry. Which reminds me, when exactly do you and Rhodri plan to get married? You've never mentioned a date.'

'Plenty of time before you need start worrying about another wedding.' Sarah jumped up to clear the table as a diversion, hideously guilty at the prospect of her mother's bitter disappointment when she learned there was to *be* no other wedding.

Sarah was ready well before the appointed hour, poised to cope with whatever mood Rupert might be in, determined not to let herself get embroiled in anything personal this time, come what may. She felt rather pleased with her detachment, but after more than half an hour of hanging about, waiting, she began to get irritable.

'Mr Clare's late,' her mother informed her unnecessarily. 'You might as well have some coffee.'

Before the coffee had time to percolate there was a screech of tyres in the drive followed by a peremptory ring of the doorbell.

'Would you put another cup out, Mother,' Sarah

called, and went to open the door, to find Rupert leaning against the lintel, blood streaming down his face through the fingers he held clamped against his cheek. Sarah looked at him aghast.

'Rupert! What happened—come in, for heaven's sake. Have you crashed the car?'

'Would you believe a misguided errand of mercy?' he said bitterly. 'For God's sake lead me to a bathroom before I bleed over your mother's carpet.'

'Mr Clare!' Mrs Morgan emerged from the kitchen, her face concerned. 'What on earth have you done to yourself! Sarah, take him into the cloakroom and see to his face, poor boy. I'll get some of your father's brandy.'

In the tiny cloakroom converted from a closet under the stairwell the 'poor boy' was in much closer quarters to Sarah than she liked as Rupert leaned against the washbasin while she examined the damage. Three vicious scratches scored one lean, brown cheek, the blood flowing freely as Sarah bathed them in water laced with antiseptic.

'Won't you kiss it better, darling?' Rupert's eyes glinted down at her shuttered face as she worked.

'I think some lint and plaster will be more use.' Sarah refused to let him unsettle her, glad that the door was half open into the hall, nevertheless very conscious of the warmth that was emanating from his body to hers. Her fingers shook slightly as she applied the final piece of plaster, and Rupert captured them, kissing them, taking the tip of each finger separately into his mouth and biting gently before releasing her hand. She stared at him mutely, then turned away to replace the dressings in the cabinet over the basin.

'Come into the drawing room and tell us what happened,' Sarah said gently, and led the way across the hall, Rupert followed close behind, taking her arm.

'Sarah——' he began, but was frustrated by the arrival of Mrs Morgan from the kitchen with a coffee tray.

'Sit down on the sofa and drink this, Mr Clare,' she

instructed briskly, and handed him a glass of brandy. 'How did you cut your face?'

'It was scratched, Mother,' said Sarah, yielding to Rupert's hand when it drew her down to sit beside him. She gave him a wicked little grin. 'The thing is, Rupert, who scratched you?'

'Not who, Sarah. What! Ah, thank you, Mrs Morgan.' He drank the spirit gratefully before going on. 'I stopped the car on the verge a short way back along the road— near the driveway to Cwmderwen Court.' He gave an ironic nod in Sarah's direction. 'Home of your fiancé, I presume?'

She inclined her head serenely and drank her coffee, ignoring the challenging look on Rupert's face. 'Do go on, Rupert,' she said calmly.

He scowled.

'I was taking some shots of the view from that point— quite superb the light and shade on those hills at this hour. The house was no use, of course, too modern for Henry V's time, but the countryside itself can't have looked all that much different in his day.'

'Tell us what happened,' said Sarah impatiently.

Rupert put a hand to his cheek, a wry grin on his face. 'I heard this God-awful—sorry, Mrs Morgan—infernal howling coming from the trees edging the road. Being a mere ignorant city dweller I thought some creature was in mortal agony and felt compelled to investigate. After a search I located the sufferer, an enormous grey Persian cat with eyes like orange-rind, howling in what I took to be terror way up high in an oak tree. Like an idiot I decided to rescue the misbegotten beast. I climbed up the tree——'

'In white drill trousers,' murmured Sarah, shaking her head.

'Having foolishly omitted to bring along a change of clothing,' agreed Rupert with asperity. 'It took me quite some time to get high enough to reach the cat. When I finally tried to get hold of the stupid beast it hissed, spat and raked its dirty great talons down my face, then scooted down the tree like a monkey and disappeared into the woods. I was left with egg on my face—not to mention blood!'

Both Mrs Morgan and Sarah were laughing by the end of Rupert's account.

'Cats are notorious creatures for disdaining help, Mr Clare.' Mrs Morgan rose as the doorbell rang. 'I know the identity of your assailant, what's more. I'm afraid it could only be Darius, Lady Marian's cat, from your description. Do excuse me—someone wanting my husband, I expect.'

As the door closed behind her Rupert held out his cup for more coffee. Sarah smiled a little maliciously as she returned it to him.

'Never mind, Rupert, you'll survive. Your tetanus shots are up to date, I know.'

Rupert laughed shortly. 'The animal might be rabid— I might have known it came from the Lloyd-Ellis household; probably acting on your swain's instructions.'

Sarah controlled a sudden urge to follow Darius's example and rake her nails down Rupert's uninjured cheek. 'You know nothing about Rhodri,' she snapped.

'All I know is that he's suddenly annexed my woman,' he said through clenched teeth, his eyes hard.

Sarah stared at him, arrested. 'That's not true. . . .'

'Isn't it? Then why were you there at the wedding with that damn' great bauble on your finger, and the highly eligible Mr Lloyd-Ellis stuck to you like glue, looking like some bloody pop-star in his white suit and his dark glasses?'

Sarah looked at him with dislike. 'Don't be childish, Rupert. His suit was beige, not white, and the glasses were necessary to hide a black eye.'

'Makes a habit of trespassing on other men's property, does he?' Rupert grinned evilly, but Sarah ignored him and poured herself more coffee, her hands shaking a little with sheer temper. 'Rhodri was merely doing me a completely disinterested kindness, if it's possible for you to understand such a thing.'

Rupert hooted. 'Oh I understand well enough, sweetheart. But don't kid yourself. He's no more disinterested than I am!'

'He's an old friend——' Sarah turned on him fiercely.

'And would like to be a lot more, from what I could see.' Rupert leaned forward, his face intimidating. 'Can you honestly swear, Sarah Morgan, that during the course of last weekend the disinterested Mr Lloyd-Ellis never made one move to cash in on his good deed?'

Colour rose in Sarah's cheeks and her eyes fell away from her inquisitor's. There was a nasty little silence, then Rupert leapt to his feet and stood glowering at her. 'I thought not!' He passed the back of his hand across his forehead, and licked his lips, blinking. Sarah looked up at him in alarm. 'It's hot in here,' he muttered, then cast a hunted glance at her, his face suddenly like clay. 'I feel a bit sickish—excuse. . . .' Before he could finish what he was saying he swayed and collapsed on the carpet with a thud, just missing the coffee tray, but overturning a small rush-bottomed chair as he went down.

'Rupert!' Sarah fell on her knees beside him, turning him over to examine his unconscious face, looking up in anguish as her parents rushed through the door.

'He fainted, Dad! You don't faint from just a scratch or two!'

'Now keep calm, Sarah, let me have a look at him.' Glyn Morgan very gently ran his fingers through the thick brown hair of the unconscious man and withdrew them slowly, sticky with blood, to the concern of both his wife and daughter.

'Glyn!' exclaimed Mrs Morgan. 'The cat can't have scratched him there as well.'

'No, indeed. He has a nasty contusion at the back of his head.' The Rector eyed his white-faced daughter with concern. 'Go and ring the doctor, Sarah, the number's on the pad by the telephone.' He looked at his wife questioningly, but she shook her head slightly as Sarah ran from the room, motioning him to be quiet. Together they managed to slide a small cushion beneath Rupert's head, but otherwise left him alone to Sarah's indignation when she flew back into the room.

'Why have you left him on the floor? I'll help to get him on the sofa——'

'No, Sarah,' said Mrs Morgan practically. 'Better to leave him where he is until the doctor sees him in case——'

'In case what?'

Her father frowned at his surprisingly impassioned daughter. 'He may have injured himself in falling, child, that's all. Did you get Dr Rowlands?'

Sarah nodded, on her knees again by Rupert.

'Just caught him before he started out on his rounds. He's on his way.' She looked up anxiously. 'He's so still—shouldn't he be coming round?'

Mrs Morgan picked up the tray, frowning slightly at her husband. 'I expect he knocked himself a bit getting down the tree, darling. Now run upstairs and get a blanket while I make some tea for us. Your father will stay with Mr Clare.'

'But——' Sarah got to her feet unwillingly, not taking her eyes off Rupert's still, pale face.

'Go on, cariad,' urged her father. 'We'd better keep him warm, do as your mother says.'

Sarah sprinted up the stairs, stripped the fluffy cellular blanket from her own bed and ran back down with it, tucking it round Rupert's inert body with unconscious tenderness. She looked up at her father with dread in her eyes.

'It can't be just a faint, surely?'

'I'm no doctor, cariad,' he answered. 'But I'm fairly sure Mr Clare is suffering from delayed concussion. He probably had a fall from the tree. Beth says Lady Marian's Darius was the cause of all this.'

Sarah scrambled to her feet as Mrs Morgan returned with a cup of tea. 'Any sign of the doctor, Mam?'

'Not yet, love. Drink this while it's hot—you're shivering.' Mrs Morgan's eyes were troubled as she handed her daughter a cup of tea. She looked down at Rupert's still face anxiously.

Sarah was surprised to realise she was indeed shivering. The hot tea helped a little, but her teeth chattered against the cup so conspicuously she put it down, jumping to her feet in relief as the doorbell rang. She raced out of the room to open the door to Dr Rowlands, an old friend from the time of her own accident. Sarah literally pushed him into the drawing room at top-speed, rapidly explaining what had happened to Rupert, giving him no time to greet her parents in her agitation. Rupert began to regain consciousness while the doctor was examining him. His dazed eyes stared blankly at the strange face bending over him, and he struggled to sit up. Dr Rowlands kept him where he was with a restraining hand.

'Steady on, old chap,' he said soothingly. 'Head aching? Nauseated? Stay where you are for a minute, you'll soon feel better.'

'Sarah——' said Rupert hoarsely, his head turning anxiously to look for her.

'I'm here, Rupert,' she said, suddenly cool.' Do stop fussing and do as you're told.'

He subsided at once, submitting to the doctor's ministrations without another word. Standing a little apart, Sarah's parents exchanged blank looks. Their daughter's change of attitude was bewildering. All the time Rupert had been unconscious Sarah had seemed wild with anxiety, yet now he was fully awake again she was cold and noticeably curt towards him. Glyn Morgan regarded Sarah's carefully controlled features with misgivings he knew very well were shared by his wife, but he put them aside in the ensuing arrangements for the invalid's comfort.

Protest as he might, Rupert was soon lying in the rectory's cool spare bedroom in an old pair of Gareth's pyjamas, with the curtains drawn against the bright sunlight, and was left in peace to drift off into a natural, healing sleep. After listening to the parting instructions from the doctor on how to care for the invalid, and on various signs to look out for should he feel worse, the

Morgans repaired to the kitchen to eat a light lunch. Sarah eyed the poached egg in front of her with marked lack of enthusiasm, but a certain familiar militancy about her mother suggested it might be easier to eat it than argue.

'Mr Clare must stay here until he's well, of course,' stated Mrs Morgan. Her husband nodded in agreement.

'I'll have a word with him when he wakes, then I'll pop into Monmouth and fetch his things.' He cast an eye at Sarah. 'Have you had some sort of disagreement with Mr Clare, my dear?'

'Why should you think that?' Sarah returned his look with one of limpid innocence.

'There is a certain aggression in your manner towards him, yet you were half-demented when the poor man collapsed.'

Sarah's face grew warm, and she turned her attention to cutting up the toast on her plate with finicking precision.

'We did have a slight difference of opinion in London,' she said carefully. 'But since I've worked with him for some time surely it was fairly natural to be concerned when he fell in a heap on the floor right at my feet. I would have felt the same whoever it was.' This was sheer prevarication, and uncomfortably aware that her parents knew this only too well, Sarah steered the conversation to the matter of looking after the unexpected patient.

'I had a word with Dr Rowlands as I saw him out,' said her father. 'The remainder of today in bed should do the trick though he advises an X-ray tomorrow to be on the safe side. And of course Mr Clare won't be able to drive for several days.'

Great, thought Sarah despondently. The last thing she wanted was Rupert under the same roof for even a few hours, let alone days, especially in the room next to hers. The morning's events had made one thing crystal clear to her. The love she felt for Rupert was very much alive, however much she told herself to the contrary, apparently totally unaffected by any of the strains put upon it. Sarah sighed as she left her mother and father in the kitchen and wandered aimlessly out into the garden to sit in the sun with a book, and stayed there until she heard Mari-Sîan arrive home from school. Her young sister was in the kitchen when Sarah went in, listening wide-eyed to her mother's account of Rupert's mishap. She rounded on Sarah in excitement.

'How amazing, Sal. What luck!'

'Depends on what you think of as luck. He should have left the cat alone.'

Sarah lifted the lid of the pan of soup simmering on the stove and inspected the contents.

'No, silly! I mean fancy having Rupert Clare in the bedroom right next to yours!'

Mrs Morgan regarded her youngest child with cold disapproval. 'I fail to see how that can affect Sarah.'

'Oh come off it, Mam.' Mari-Sîan gave a horrific leer at Sarah. 'Pity the floorboards are so noisy in this house.'

'Mari-Sîan! Go upstairs and change your clothes quickly, then come and have tea.'

'Joke, Mam, joke,' said Mari-Sîan pacifically, then spoiled it by asking if she could take the tray up to Rupert.

'Certainly not,' said her mother tartly. 'Now go.'

'Why should Sarah have all the fun?' Mari-Sîan grinned unrepentantly and whirled round to collide with her father. 'Sorry, Dad.'

'Your mother or I will attend to our guest,' said the Rector, with a gentle reproof in his voice that vanquished his lively child instantly, and she made a hurried escape. The Morgan offspring always found their father's forbearance ten times harder to bear than their mother's temper.

'Has Rupert been asleep all the time?' asked Sarah casually.

'Yes.' Mrs Morgan sounded short. 'Your father will have to disturb him now to ask for his car-keys. Glyn can't get out with the Metro in the drive, and he's going into Monmouth to collect Mr Clare's things from the hotel and tell them what happened.'

There was little point in trying to avoid the subject of their visitor over afternoon tea, as Mari-Sîan was bubbling with curiosity about him and kept on *ad nauseam*. Apparently he had merely surfaced long enough to indicate the whereabouts of the keys before going back to sleep without drinking any of the tea his host had taken him.

'He's likely to be thirsty when he wakes,' said the Rector as he left. 'Keep an eye on him.'

'No sweat, Dad,' called Mari-Sîan, giggling at her father's distaste as he frowned at her on his way out.

'You keep well away from Mr Clare's room,' warned her mother. 'He won't want you about the place if he's feeling ill.'

'I'd be surprised if he wanted any of us,' said Sarah. 'Rupert's hardly the most biddable of people when he's under the weather.'

Her mother looked at her suspiciously. 'Have you looked after him before, then?'

'No. He has a very efficient housekeeper, Mother. I just do his typing.' There was a certain little air of dignity about Sarah as she cleared the table that put an end to any further remarks on the subject, and the other two began to talk of the summer fête due to take place at the Court the following Saturday.

'Lady Marian will be away, of course, but will Rhodri be here for it?' asked Mrs Morgan.

'Possibly,' said Sarah, privately resolved to keep him away by brute force if necessary. The thought of any more public appearances together as an engaged couple gave her private hysterics. Sarah retired to her room, determined to sort it out with Rhodri at the first possible opportunity, suddenly sick and shabby-feeling about the entire business. She glared malevolently at the guest-room door as she passed. It was all Rupert's fault. He was at the bottom of all her troubles. If he hadn't behaved like a sex-starved lecher none of this need be happening. He could be occupying that same room as her future husband instead of temporary patient, not to mention permanent thorn in her flesh. In frustration Sarah flung into her room and threw herself down on her bed, all at once utterly exhausted and disinclined for company. She was still there, fast asleep, when her mother came upstairs an hour later, to check on Rupert.

Mrs Morgan looked at the unconscious male profile of her guest, dark against the white sheets, then went to gaze at the crumpled little heap on the bed next door. Tentatively she put out a hand to stroke the glossy tangle of hair, then withdrew it quickly as Sarah stirred, muttering a little before snuggling deeper into the pillows with a sigh.

Rupert Clare continued to sleep. He lay like the dead, long after Sarah woke from her nap and began to help her mother with dinner. In an agony of anxiety at Rupert's protracted slumbers, not daring to investigate as she longed to do, she contented herself with the bulletins given at intervals by her mother in her self-imposed role of nurse.

'It will do him the world of good,' said Mrs Morgan with emphasis, by no means unaware of the worry secretly burning inside her silent daughter.

'It seems so odd, I suppose,' said Sarah, striving for a neutral tone. 'Rupert normally never needs much sleep—he does most of his dictating at night.'

'His system is no doubt taking advantage of the opportunity,' said Glyn Morgan. 'He'll probably sleep right through the night.'

To Sarah's dismay his prediction proved to be accurate. When it came to the normal hour for bed in the Rectory there was no sign of stirring from the occupant of the guest room.

'Do you think he's all right?' whispered Sarah on the landing after her mother had made a final check on Rupert before retiring.

'Yes, I do,' answered Mrs Morgan firmly, and pushed her through the doorway of her own room. 'Now go to sleep yourself, Sarah—you look very tired. Don't worry,

I'll hear Mr Clare if he wakes.'

Uneasily Sarah undressed and got into bed, staring out through the open lattice at the moonlit night sky, feeling tense and restless, utterly disinclined for sleep after her rest earlier. She let out a sigh of exasperation and slid off the bed to stand at the small window, remaining there for a long time while what breeze there was cooled her skin sufficiently through the flimsy lawn of her nightdress for her to face the thought of returning to bed. Eventually she lay down again, but it was well into the night before she drifted away into a half-world somewhere between waking and sleeping.

When Sarah woke with a start she had no way of telling what time it was. The house was silent, and the earlier moonlight had given way to a warm, dense darkness. Her heart beat thickly as if some sound had startled her awake, and she sat up, swinging her feet quietly to the floor. Faint, unidentifiable sounds reached her from the next room and Sarah stole on noiseless bare feet to see what was troubling Rupert.

She hesitated in the doorway to his room, then closed the door softly behind her and tip-toed in the darkness to the bed, where Rupert was thrashing about wildly, incoherent mutterings coming from his throat as he wrestled with what seemed to be a nightmare. Sarah laid a cool hand on his forehead, almost tripping as she leaned over him, her feet tangling in what felt like a discarded pyjama jacket on the floor.

'Hush, Rupert,' she whispered urgently. His forehead was hot beneath her fingers, his hair damp where it lay across his forehead in a sweat-soaked tangle. 'It's all right. Just a dream.' He moved restlessly, one arm flailing in a sweep that would have floored her if it had connected. Sarah grabbed his hand and shook it slightly.

'Hey. Wake up. It's Sarah—everything's fine. Calm down.'

Abruptly he was still. His breathing slowed, and the hand she was holding tightened on hers, the long fingers curling round her own.

'Sarah?' he muttered uncertainly. 'Are you a dream?'

'No. You were making very strange noises, so I came to investigate—a minor nightmare by the sound of it.'

'I was being sacrificed.' He still sounded breathless. 'A great crowd of people were forcing me up a steep slope to a great flat stone at the top, and they pushed me off—I was falling——' Some of the horror obviously still remained with him as a great shudder went through him, like a small boy afraid of the dark.

'Let my hand go now.' Sarah made her voice deliberately prosaic.

'Could I just hang on to it for a moment, Nanny?' Something of Rupert's normal bantering tone was returning, to Sarah's relief.

'I'm bent over in a very uncomfortable position, Rupert, my back's aching.'

'Then come in here with me,' he whispered promptly, and tugged on her hand.

'Obviously you're back to normal,' she said coldly, and tried to free herself. 'For heaven's sake, Rupert, let me up.'

For answer he merely pulled harder and Sarah collapsed on the bed, half-lying on top of him. In an instant both his arms were round her and she was a prisoner, held fast against his chest.

'Stay a moment, Sarah,' he whispered. 'I still feel disorientated. I was actually falling through space—God, it was spine-chilling.'

'Man's oldest fear,' Sarah said indistinctly, and tried to pull away, every nerve-end aware of Rupert's bare chest, the warm, rumpled bed, her family sleeping close at hand, and above all the intimacy of their situation in the hot darkness, with his iron grip holding her immobile except for the quickened tempo of her breathing. Refusing to panic Sarah said reasonably,

'If I stay a minute or so will you promise to let me go then, Rupert?'

'Five minutes,' he breathed in her ear. The breath was hot against her skin, and a sudden thrill of apprehension curled through her.

'My parents——' she began apprehensively.

'Asleep. So don't run the risk of waking them, darling.' His voice was barely audible, his whisper so close against her neck it was a caress. I am a fool, thought Sarah with clarity. I should be struggling like mad, fighting to preserve my virtue, letting him know I'm no pushover, even if he is sick. She knew very well that it was high time to go, but, quiet as he was, his arms were unrelenting in their grasp. Weakly her rigid body relaxed a little against him. For long minutes they lay motionless, then before she knew what he was doing, Rupert removed the sheet that separated her body from his and slid it over them both, wrapping them in an enclosed, private little world.

'Rupert!' Sarah was burningly aware that not only his pyjama jacket lay on the floor. The frail barrier of her nightdress was all that separated them as their bodies came into contact. 'No! Please—I must go,' she whispered fiercely, trying to twist away, but Rupert merely held her closer, burying his face in her neck, one arm restraining her, his other hand stroking her back delicately, gentling her to a state of acquiescence, reassured to passivity by the slowing movements of a hand that grew heavy, as heavy as Sarah's eyelids as she relaxed against Rupert's body, drowsy and supine, knowing she must leave in a moment or two. In just a moment more she would slide out of his hold, even now his caressing hand was almost still, and finally it lay immobile and heavy between her shoulder blades and Rupert slept.

CHAPTER SEVEN

SARAH woke slowly. It took some time for her to realise that her head rested on something far different from her usual pillow. To her consternation she was still held close in Rupert's arms, her face against the smooth skin of his broad chest and worse, it was late. Sunshine was filtering through the drawn damask curtains. Rupert muttered indistinctly into her hair and tightened his arm as she struggled to release herself. Sarah freed a hand and pushed at his chest.

'Wake up—let me go. It's morning,' she whispered.

'Darling,' he muttered, his eyes still closed, and sighing he settled his long body more comfortably against hers. Sarah yanked on his ear and his eyes flew open.

'Vixen,' he said amiably, smiling lazily at her, then his eyes looked over her bare shoulder and became fixed.

Sarah twisted wildly in Rupert's hold and turned over in foreboding. Her mother stood in the open doorway, a tray in her hands, her eyes filled with sick shock and pain as they dropped from the entwined figures on the bed to the discarded pyjamas lying on the carpet. Without a word she put down the tray on a chair near the door and withdrew hastily, face averted, closing the door with a positive click that galvanised Sarah into life.

'Mother!' She leaped from the bed, but Rupert caught her hand and pulled her back, forcing her to sit on the edge of it. Her blue eyes blazed at him with white hot fury. 'Let me go and explain——'

'Explain what?' Rupert's eyes were expressionless green glass as he leaned back against the pillows, his fingers like a manacle on her wrist. 'In my experience, circumstantial evidence is what most people go by, Sarah, as you should know. However much you explain to your mother that your motives in visiting me were purely altruistic and that my motive in keeping you with me was a burning need for *com*passion rather than passion, she will see in her mind's eye the picture we presented as she opened the door.'

Sarah pulled away from him, sitting with shoulders hunched and head bowed in an agony of sick distaste, all her emotions welded together into a cold fury directed against the man in the bed, who was explaining with cool reason what her brain recognised as all too true. She turned her head and looked at him dully.

'You will at least support my explanation, Rupert?'

He returned her look steadily. 'Why should I, Sarah? Under circumstances of a similar nature you gave me no chance at all to explain, let alone the opportunity for corroboration from Naomi.'

Sarah's head lifted proudly. 'The case is slightly different. My parents know I'm not indiscriminate——'

'You mean they believe you are not.'

'It's the same thing; stop splitting hairs.' Sarah stood up, hugging her arms around herself in misery, indifferent to the fact that she was wearing only a nightgown. She glared at Rupert with dislike. '*You* were in bed with your former mistress and besides, your reputation is well known.'

Rupert heaved himself up against the headboard, arranging the bedclothes modestly over his lower half with an elaborate care that set Sarah's teeth on edge.

'Your distress is distorting your judgment, Sarah, and you so good at sifting out fact from fiction as a rule! I was *not* in bed with Naomi, and my reputation is largely a matter of conjecture and publicity. Give a dog a bad name and all that. You believe what you *assumed* to be the truth. A good thing you never considered studying for the Bar.'

'It's not your problem I'm concerned about at the moment—it's mine,' she snapped. Their eyes remained locked for several moments, until Rupert's dropped to the outline of her body through the thin white lawn, and Sarah burned with sudden awareness, making precipitately for the door. She turned with desperate appeal on her face, her eyes imploring.

'Please tell them nothing happened, Rupert.'

'I'll say all the right things. Don't worry,' he said calmly, 'I'm getting up.'

How could she not worry, thought Sarah miserably as she took a hasty bath and flung on jeans and a shirt before going downstairs to confront her parents. The door from the hall into the kitchen was closed, and Sarah's hand shook as she turned the big brass knob and went into the silent, sunlit room. Her father and mother sat quietly, an untouched cup of tea in front of each of them on the big square table.

'Mam ... Dad ...' Sarah faltered as they turned towards her. There was no condemnation on either face. Her father's ascetic features held an expression of bewildered resignation, while her mother seemed drained of all her normal vivacity, her eyes sliding away from Sarah's in pained embarrassment as she rose to her feet. 'I'd better take some breakfast up to Mr Clare then,' she said, turning away.

'No.' Sarah swallowed. 'I mean he's coming down in a minute.'

'I see.' Mrs Morgan sat down again and took a sip from her cup.

'One gathers Mr Clare is feeling considerably better?' Her father's dry tone brought a rush of colour to Sarah's cheeks. She threw out her hands imploringly.

'It wasn't at all as you think—truly!' To her horror both her parents visibly withdrew. 'Mam, Dad, it's the truth. Nothing happened.'

'Don't be silly, girl,' snapped Mrs Morgan, her colour high. 'How you behave is your own business, after all.' She wiped her eyes fiercely with a handkerchief. 'I would prefer you not to repeat—that sort of thing in my own house, however.'

'It wasn't "that sort of thing",' said Sarah in desperation.

'Do you think I was born yesterday?' Mrs Morgan

eyed her with distaste. 'You and that man were—were wrapped around each other in bed and, well, he wasn't wearing any pyjamas!' She whisked away to put on the kettle.

Sarah gave up. She sat down next to her father, who remained silent, avoiding her beseeching eyes. Apart from Mrs Morgan's noisy clashing of crockery there was silence in the room, heavy and fraught with suppressed emotion.

'So you intend to condemn me unheard,' said Sarah quietly at last. Her father put out a hand to cover hers instantly, shaking his head as he met her eyes with compassion.

'We would never condemn, Sarah, you are our child. Whatever you do we shall always love you—and forgive.'

At his words such a lost, forlorn look dawned in Sarah's eyes Glyn Morgan's heart was wrung. 'Cariad——' he began, only to be interrupted.

'I did warn you, Sarah.'

All three turned to look at Rupert as he stood there, hands in the pockets of his cream cotton trousers, the olive green of his silk shirt accentuating the colour of his eyes as they moved from one face to another. He came into the kitchen and pulled up a chair close to Sarah's.

'What would you like for breakfast, Mr Clare?' Beth Morgan asked punctiliously.

'I've no wish to trouble you, Mrs Morgan,' he said smoothly.

'A bit late for that,' she said bluntly. 'Now. You've eaten nothing for the past twenty-four hours. I let no one go hungry under my roof, so what will you have?'

Rupert capitulated gracefully. 'In that case a piece of toast and some black coffee would be welcome.'

'Surely you can do better than that, Mr Clare!' The Rector looked distressed, and shot a quelling glance towards his hostile wife.

'No, really, that's all I need.' Rupert took one of Sarah's hands in his. 'What are *you* eating?'

Sarah looked at him numbly, then shook her head. 'I'm not hungry.'

Mrs Morgan bit her lip as she saw her daughter's colourless face. 'Now don't be silly—you must have something.'

Sarah shrugged indifferently. 'Coffee, then. It really doesn't matter.'

There was an interval while Mrs Morgan made coffee and toast and her husband asked polite questions on Rupert's health and reminded him of the suggested X-ray. Sarah sat quietly during the civilised interchange, only coming to life when her mother put a steaming cup of coffee in front of her and pressed her to eat something. Sarah obediently chewed on a piece of unwanted toast, while Rupert ate several slices with apparent enjoyment, a fact which injected a small surge of resentment into Sarah's apathy. When Rupert had finished his second cup of coffee he looked from the Rector to Mrs Morgan, his gaze resting longest on Sarah's bowed head beside him.

'Now, Sarah,' he said in a business-like manner that brought her eyes up to his sharply. 'Let us give your parents the true version of our relationship.'

Glyn Morgan stiffened. 'Mr Clare, there really is no need.'

'On the contrary, Rector. I think there's every need.' Rupert's smooth voice turned to steel as he continued. 'Sarah's distress is obvious, also there is my own position as a guest under your roof. Added to both of these is a regrettably petty urge to be more generous towards your daughter than she was to me under very similar circumstances.'

Sarah looked at him suspiciously. 'Rupert——'

'It's all right, darling,' he said soothingly, increasing the bewilderment on both senior Morgan faces. 'Let's indulge in a little mutual clarification. You first.'

Sarah frowned, by no means clear as to how much he wanted her to tell. 'I don't think this is necessary.'

Her parents watched, fascinated, as their daughter and her employer stared at each other in a clash of wills which Sarah eventually lost.

'Where shall I start?' she asked eventually, giving in.

'From your phonecall to your mother before the wedding to your arrival home, I think.' Rupert smiled his thanks as Mrs Morgan refilled his coffee cup and sat, relaxed, as Sarah reluctantly embarked on her account of what happened.

To their eternal credit her parents kept silent throughout Sarah's unembellished little story, though plainly startled when she reached the scene in Rupert's bedroom, but the part that brought violent reaction from Mrs Morgan was when she realised Sarah's engagement had been to Rupert Clare and not Rhodri Lloyd-Ellis. As Sarah finished with how Rhodri had impulsively cast himself in the role of her fiancé as a face-saving mission Mrs Morgan could keep quiet no longer.

'So you deceived us about that too, Sarah!' Red spots burned in her cheeks. 'We shall be laughing-stocks in the village!'

The Rector looked at his wife in disapproval, his eyes icy.

'It was not Sarah who deceived us, Beth, but Rhodri, and the opinions of other people are the least of our considerations.' His wife had the grace to look ashamed and subsided, leaving her husband to touch his daughter's hand gently. 'Now tell us what happened last night, cariad.'

Sarah was silent for a moment. She knew only too well why Rupert had insisted on her telling the truth. This was his way of underlining how easy it was to accept the sometimes doubtful evidence of one's own eyes, however mistaken. She hesitated, knowing just how much her parents wanted to be convinced that there were extenuating circumstances for the scene Mrs Morgan had interrupted. She looked up at Rupert. There was no evasion in his answering gaze, and suddenly Sarah remembered something overlooked in the heat of her blind, unreasoning reaction to the scene in his bedroom. Whatever else he might be, Rupert was no liar. He had volunteered no explanation for what had happened, it was true, wanting her to believe in him implicitly, without explanations. He had expected faith and trust, and she had been utterly unable to give him either.

'I think it might be a good idea if we heard Rupert's side of what happened in St John's Wood,' she said carefully. 'You've heard what I saw. I realise now it's only fair to hear his story.'

'Quite right, my dear,' said her father approvingly.

'Thank you.' Rupert inclined his head in acknowledgement, and began. Sarah listened with head bent, intent on his every word as the detached, dispassionate voice gave a laconic account of the events that led up to Sarah's dramatic entrance into his bedroom on that memorable morning.

Unknown to Sarah, Naomi Prentiss, Rupert's former fiancée, had married an up-and-coming theatrical producer some six months previously, but the marriage had been kept secret, its announcement timed for the opening of *Crown in Jeopardy* in the West End, starring Naomi, and written and produced by her husband.

'I knew this, of course,' said Rupert. 'Naomi and I have remained friends even though a marriage was not a viable prospect. I'm still fond of her, and she's still fond of me. We like each other much more this way.'

Sarah looked at him speculatively, but he kept his face turned towards her parents.

'Go on, Mr Clare.' Mrs Morgan was obviously interested. 'Let's hear the rest.'

'Naomi and Theo went on a short trip to the States last week, sounding out the possibilities of a Broadway run after the West End,' he continued. 'While they were away the Press got wind of the marriage and were there at the airport in full force when they got back. Naomi is the world's worst traveller and had been ill on the flight, as usual, so to get away from the reporters they came to my house instead of returning to Theo's flat. To cut a long story short, they were both suffering from jet-lag, and after dinner needed little coaxing to accept my offer of a bed. My bed; I slept in the spare room.' Rupert swivelled his head to look Sarah full in the eye. 'When you arrived I had just taken them in a tray of coffee, and was collecting my shaver from my bathroom, where Theo was in the process of taking a bath. End of story.'

Sarah was assailed by so many conflicting emotions she felt dizzy. Joy, remorse, guilt and relief all struggled hard for supremacy as she looked unhappily at Rupert.

'I'm sorry.' She knew it sounded lame and inadequate, but felt shy of saying anything more heartfelt with her parents looking on.

'You were a bit silly, to my mind, Sarah,' her mother commented, 'going off half-cocked like that. Not like you at all.'

'One *can* over-react sometimes,' said Sarah gently, her meaning unmistakable.

Mrs Morgan bridled, flushing slightly. 'I think *I* had a good right to be upset, my girl!'

'Of course, Mrs Morgan,' put in Rupert smoothly. He smiled at Sarah encouragingly. 'Go on, round it off. Tell your parents how you came to be in the wrong bed this morning.'

Glyn Morgan cleared his throat, his colour high. 'If Sarah finds this embarrassing——'

'No, Dad.' Sarah smiled at him lovingly. 'You do, I know, but hear me out.' Quickly she told how Rupert's cries had disturbed her.

'When she arrived at my bedside she found I'd reverted to childhood, scared stiff by a nightmare where I was falling through space. I insisted on her staying a while until I got back to normal,' Rupert continued. He looked very directly from the Rector to Mrs Morgan. 'At which interesting point, however, much against us as it may have looked, we fell asleep, and that was how you found us in the morning, Mrs Morgan.'

'Well, that's all right, then,' said Mrs Morgan briskly, patently glad to change the subject. She jumped to her feet, 'I must be off now, I'm due at the WI Garden Club meeting in ten minutes. Are you taking Mr Clare to the hospital, Glyn?'

'I'm sure it isn't necessary,' said Rupert at once. 'I've slept off any ill-effects, apart from a bit of a bump on my head as a memento of—what did you say the cat was called?'

'Darius Lloyd-Ellis,' said the Rector with a twinkle. 'And I think you ought to have the X-ray just the same— if only to avoid any nightmares in future.'

Rupert smiled back, an answering glint in his own eyes. 'Very well, sir, if you can spare the time. But I assure you there's no likelihood of any nocturnal recurrences.' There was mutual understanding in the look the two men exchanged, but Mrs Morgan, speedily washing plates with Sarah's assistance, brought up a subject which was obviously causing her a great deal of concern.

'If you'll forgive just one question,' she said tartly, 'to whom, exactly, *are* you engaged, Sarah, if anyone, as far as the world is concerned?'

'For world you mean WI,' said Sarah with a grin.

'Your father may be above such secular trivialities, being a man of the cloth, but as Rector's wife I'm involved in everything that goes on in Cwmderwen.' Mrs Morgan gave a final swipe of her snowy dishcloth on the already gleaming draining-board. 'People are bound to talk about you, Sarah.'

'Which is hardly a novelty, Mother!' Sarah lost patience. 'Tell them what you like, I really don't care.'

It was left to Rupert to pour oil on troubled waters.

'Why don't you leave things as they are for the time being,' he suggested. 'If someone asks about the wedding date, Mrs Morgan, just say Sarah's giving you a breathing space after Rhia. Then Sarah—or Lloyd-Ellis—can break the so-called engagement at a later date when things have blown over a bit.'

Sarah felt irrationally nettled at Rupert's cool advice, even though it was the precise idea she'd had in mind herself.

'I'm perfectly capable of organising my own life, thank you,' she said cuttingly.

Rupert's face darkened. 'One could be forgiven for doubting it after the events of the recent few days.' He turned to her father in apology. 'If this is your most convenient time to play chauffeur, I'm in your hands, Rector. Goodbye for now, Mrs Morgan.' He looked at Sarah levelly. 'I'll see you later.'

'Why didn't you go with them, Sarah?' asked her mother as the two men left the house.

'I wasn't asked.' Sarah turned away. 'I'll tidy the house while you're out at your meeting, Mother.'

'Sarah.'

She turned at the anxious note in her mother's voice. Elizabeth Morgan smiled uncertainly as she met Sarah's uncompromising blue gaze.

'I'm sorry I thought the worst when I found you——'

'*In flagrante?*' Sarah shrugged. 'Who am I to judge, Mother—I jumped to the wrong conclusion about Rupert, after all, and look at the fuss *that* has caused, one way and another!'

Mrs Morgan took off her apron and followed Sarah up the stairs.

'In extenuation,' she said to her daughter's straight back, 'one only feels so enraged where one loves. It's very much easier to take an impartial view where the emotions aren't involved.'

Sarah thought that one over carefully when she was alone in the house. She occupied herself with making beds, disentangling the rat's nest Mari-Sîan had made of her bedroom, dusting and pushing the vaccuum-cleaner around with a desperate sort of energy, as though her hyperactivity was likely to stimulate her thinking processes. She had no idea what was expected of her now. Presumably it was tacitly assumed she was Rupert's property again instead of Rhodri's, to her mother's intense disappointment. A famous author was no substitute for the heir to Cwmderwen Court as far as Mrs Morgan was concerned, that was obvious. Sarah took a plastic container of soup from the freezer in the big, flag-stoned larder as instructed, and set the contents to thaw in a pan on the stove. Cream of courgette, she noted automatically, wondering if Rupert liked it, not caring overmuch if he didn't. She stood still in the middle of the kitchen. She was being a trifle unjust towards Rupert, if she were honest. He had been very supportive in the face of her parents' patent shock and disapproval, after all, and he had far more right to be angry with her than she had ever had with him. Sarah frowned and bit her lip. She invariably managed to do the wrong thing, it seemed.

Aware that she was allowing herself a self-indulgent wallow, Sarah shook herself impatiently and began concocting a salad from all the fresh vegetables at her disposal in the Rectory kitchen-garden. She devilled eggs and made French dressing, transferred the soup to a heated tureen, then filled the kettle, her eyes absent as she worked. Sarah was so intent on a mental reconstruction of her life she failed to hear footsteps in the hall, only aware of Rupert's presence when he came to stand behind her, his hands sliding round her waist in silence. Sarah leaned back against him without protest,

'How was the X-ray?' she asked.

'I must possess an extra tough cranium. My fall had no effect on it,' he said dryly.

'You said nothing about a fall at the time.'

'It seemed so ridiculous.'

There was silence for a while.

'Where's Father?' she asked idly.

'Gone to pick up your mother.'

Sarah felt his cheek settle on her hair, and they remained in silence, both gazing through the window.

'Something smells good,' he said quietly.

'Mother's soup. Cream of courgette.'

'Sounds tempting. Sarah.'

'M'm?'

'What now?'

'I don't know.' Sarah freed herself and turned round to face him. 'What did you have in mind?'

Rupert shook his head, his eyes grave. 'It's what *you* have in mind that concerns me, Sarah. Will you come back with me to London in a day or two, or do you want to stay here for a while?' He put out a finger and touched her bottom lip, smiling faintly. 'Or did the revelations of the morning have no bearing on your decision to desert me permanently for pastures new? Pastures that lie fairly close to home too, if that's not proving too near the mark.'

Sarah said nothing, allowing her eyes to wander feature by feature from his thick brown hair down over the deep-set eyes and belligerent nose to the wide firm-lipped mouth and assertive chin. His skin was only a shade or two lighter than his hair, an accident of pigment, not the result of hours in the sun. As Sarah knew only too well there were times when Rupert barely saw the light of day, nor had he patience to lie on a sun-bed, or whatever vainer men did to achieve the same even colour given him by some good fairy at his birth. Rupert stood motionless beneath her scrutiny, waiting for her to speak. Sarah sighed and went over to the stove, taking refuge in fussing with the soup.

'I'm not sure just exactly what I *do* want,' she said, and turned to smile at him in apology, her smile fading as she caught a fierce blaze in his eyes before he dropped his lids, quenching it. He shrugged.

'Which answers my question for me fairly comprehensively, I suppose.'

Sarah frowned. 'That's not exactly what I——' she stopped as her parents' voices sounded in the hall, and in the ensuing preparations for lunch, and her mother's amusing account of the selection of WI floral entries for the forthcoming show, any further discussion was ruled out.

Mrs Morgan had apparently decided to establish diplomatic relations as far as Rupert was concerned; whether on her husband's instructions or of her own volition Sarah was unsure. Whatever the reason her affability made lunch a more pleasant meal than breakfast, and Rupert set himself out to charm with a purpose Sarah recognised from the days when he was continuously in pursuit of some female or other. He praised the soup, helped hand round salad and cheese, asked numerous questions on Mrs Morgan's participation in the life of the village, and long before the raspberry tart was served Sarah could see her mother was completely won over.

Her father caught Sarah's eye with a wry little smile, and Sarah smiled back warmly, glad that the stunned expression of early morning was now replaced by amusement.

'Beware, Elizabeth,' he said, wagging a finger at his wife's animated face. 'Mr Clare is no doubt storing up all this information to use at some future time in print.'

'Very astute, sir.' Rupert grinned disarmingly. He included both Sarah's parents as he said, 'I'd be very pleased if you would use my first name.'

They assented willingly, while Sarah looked on in silence, secretly marvelling at the contrast between breakfast and lunch. In just a short time Rupert Clare had transformed himself from villain of the piece to hero of the hour in one fell swoop. She got up as the phone rang.

'I'll answer it,' she said, glad to escape from the atmosphere of bonhomie in the kitchen.

'Sal?' Mari-Sîan sounded excited. 'I was praying you'd answer.'

'Nice to be wanted, what's up?'

'Bron wants me to spend the evening with her—stay the night. Could you just nip out and ask the parents? I've got clean nether-garments, tell Mam, and it's cleared with Mrs Parry.'

Sarah looked at the phone with suspicion. 'And why should I be necessary to make such an innocent request?'

'Just ask, Sal—please. The pips will go in a minute.'

'Hang on.'

Sarah went back to the kitchen. 'Mari-Sîan requesting permission to stay the night with Bronwen—at Mrs Parry's invitation, I gather.'

Mrs Morgan nodded after raising a questioning eyebrow at her husband. 'Yes, all right, love. Does she have——?'

'Yes, she does, Mam!'

Grinning, Sarah went back to the phone. 'All clear. So tell me what you're really going to do!'

'Suspicious cow! End of term party, don't worry, I'll tell all when I come home tomorrow.'

'Not *all*, poppet, just the expurgated version!'

Mari-Sîan's giggle was cut off by the pips and Sarah returned to the kitchen to find Rupert being instructed to retire to bed for an hour or two.

'Have a heart, sir! I spent most of yesterday asleep.' Rupert put up a hand in protest.

'It's what they advised, Rupert,' said the Rector mildly, and Rupert gave in at once, smiling in rueful apology at Sarah.

'Forgive me for deserting you, but your father's determined to see I toe the line.'

'Nice change for you,' she said sweetly. 'Off to bye-byes, then.'

It was plain he would have liked to retaliate, but, conscious of her parents' presence Rupert excused himself and went upstairs. Too late Sarah realised she needed to change her clothes, but under the circumstances felt unwilling to go upstairs while Rupert was in his room. She fumed inwardly at her ridiculous feeling of embarrassment, like some Victorian housemaid caught kissing a footman.

'Why don't you lie in the sun for a bit,' suggested her mother. 'Do you good to have a rest, you look a bit tired.'

Without a trip upstairs there was no way Sarah could get into something more suitable for sunbathing.

'I feel too restless to sit about,' she said untruthfully. 'I'll do a spot of gardening instead.'

The Rector returned to his sermon while Sarah went

out to attack the weeds in the vegetable garden, applying hoe and fork with an energy that began to flag after the first hour. Her mother departed for the village, and yet more preparations for the show, a committee meeting with tea and cakes this time.

'I've done the vegetables,' she said firmly. 'There's nothing for you to do. I'll grill the trout when I get home. For heaven's sake go and have a bath and a rest.'

Sarah gave in, conscious of the sweat pouring down her face, and went indoors. She put her head round the door of the study. 'I'm going to have a bath, Dad.'

'Really?' He looked at her over his spectacles. 'Do you need to report on your whereabouts?'

To her intense annoyance Sarah went bright red. 'I just thought——'

'Sarah, really!' There was a whimsical smile on his handsome face. 'To be surprised in a man's bed once is unfortunate—twice would be criminally careless! Now don't fall asleep in the bath.'

Sarah ran upstairs lighter of heart. She might have known her father was well aware of her silly, furtive qualms. She collected a change of clothes, then had a quick look through Mari-Siân's selection of literature, some of which was rather surprising, eventually choosing *The Go-Between* to read again while she lingered in the bath. She dallied so long, drowsing in the warm, scented water, the book abandoned on the floor, that the loud knock on the door startled her awake, the water sloshing as she sat up with a start.

'Sarah?' Rupert's voice was sharp. 'Your father sent me to make sure you're awake.'

'I am now,' she called tartly. 'I'll be down in five minutes.'

'Tea awaits you out on the lawn, made by my own hands, so put a move on.'

Without waiting for her response Rupert returned downstairs, and Sarah hurriedly washed her hair and rinsed herself with cold water to wake herself up. Ten minutes later, her hair glossy and disciplined, her face lightly made-up, she went down to join the men, wearing a pink cotton sundress and feeling very much better. She thanked Rupert when he held out one of the white wrought-iron chairs for her, and sat behind the tea-tray, aware that his eyes took in her appearance with an approving warmth that did wonders for her self-esteem.

'You look very pretty this afternoon, cariad.' Her father accepted his cup of tea, smiling at her knowingly. 'I assume you did nod off in the bath?'

Sarah nodded, smiling guiltily.

'One of my failings,' she informed Rupert, who was lounging on the grass at her feet.

'What are the others, I wonder?' he said, straight faced.

'How much information have you managed to garner on Henry V's Monmouth?' asked the Rector hastily.

Rupert responded immediately, instantly absorbed as he outlined the plot for his novel, where the Lancastrian king would figure only in the background as the liege of a young nobleman in his army, whose life becomes endangered when he is accused of treasonal activities because of his love for a lady of Yorkist sympathies.

'The Lady Alinor's father is part of a Yorkist plot to put Edmund Mortimer on the throne and my hero, Piers Greville, gets entangled in a web of love and conflicting loyalties against a background tapestry of battle, seige, pestilence and brutality.' Rupert sat up, linking his hands round his knees as he warmed to his theme. 'Harry of Monmouth appears rather different from the patriotic, romantic figure of Shakespeare's play. Patriotic yes, but fanatically ambitious, riddled with guilt at his father's usurpation of the throne, and finally hounded to death by his indefatigable enemy—dysentery.' Rupert checked himself, smiling in apology. 'Forgive me, I tend to run on a bit, sir. It's the background that Sarah fills in for me so diligently. She's invaluable in providing details of the daily life of long ago.'

'Having been engaged in a similar, though far less ambitious work, myself for the past twenty years,' sighed

Glyn Morgan. 'I can well appreciate how useful such help must be.'

'Did you never enlist Sarah, sir?' asked Rupert curiously.

The other man shook his head, smiling affectionately at his daughter.

'Our little bird flew the nest very early.'

'It seemed like a good idea at the time,' murmured Sarah, her eyes on her fingers, which were industriously reducing a biscuit to crumbs on her plate. 'Have you exhausted Monmouth's possibilities, Rupert?'

'I think the rest could be done in London. I've seen the area, taken pictures, and amassed quite a few helpful leaflets on the region from the Tourist Office. One more day in the town to take in the Castle remains and I should be set up.' Rupert leaned back on his hands and looked at Sarah's averted face. 'Will you come back to town with me?'

Angered by such a loaded question in front of her father Sarah busied herself with piling the tea things on a tray, avoiding Rupert's probing look.

'I'm rather enjoying my little holiday here for the time being.' This was by no means wholly the truth, but Sarah rose calmly and picked up the tray, smiling politely as she motioned Rupert to remain where he was. 'Stay here and talk to Father—I'll lay the table for dinner after I've washed up. We'll honour you with a meal in the dining room tonight.'

The men watched her leave in silence, then resumed their conversation, as Sarah could see from the kitchen window, oddly nettled that her presence was so obviously not missed. She was annoyed with herself, hardly knowing why she felt so flat and depressed, her basic honesty finally forcing her to admit she wanted Rupert on his knees, ring in hand, imploring her to return to him, to forgive his transgression—her thoughts came skidding to a halt. Rupert had not transgressed. Presumably to his way of thinking it was Sarah who had caused all the fuss and plunged the Morgans into a morass of fabrication, not he. Rupert no doubt considered it was up to her to grovel and apologise and set things right. If so he was in for a disappointment, decided Sarah and marched into the dining room to arrange her mother's best table-mats and silver on the oak table. When she heard Rupert in the hall she squared her shoulders, ready to be maddeningly elusive in answer to any overture he might make, but as usual he took the wind out of her sails by announcing casually he was off to Monmouth for half an hour.

'Your much-tried father insists on running me in,' he said ruefully, 'which makes me feel no end of a fraud. I'm sure I'm perfectly capable of driving myself.'

'If Father was given instructions on your welfare you can be certain he'll do everything in his power to carry them out.' Even to herself Sarah sounded waspish.

Rupert eyed the martial set of her shoulders warily. 'Now if *you* could drive everything would be so much simpler,' he said mildly.

'Possibly. But I can't.' Sarah refused to meet his eyes.

'And you won't learn?'

'No. Which is hardly surprising.'

'Sarah, is something wrong?'

She lifted her chin and gave him a bright smile. 'Wrong? What could possibly be wrong? Have fun.'

Rupert stood with head tilted back, looking down his nose at her, his eyes narrowed, then he shrugged, put out a hand to touch her cheek, then went off to join her father.

Sarah stood with her hands clasped behind her back as she watched them go. Of course there was something wrong! It had apparently never occurred to Rupert that she might want to go too, instead of being left alone. Disconsolately she wandered up to the bathroom to retrieve her book, then went out into the garden to read in the sun, forlorn as a child deprived of a treat, and heartily glad when her mother came home to dispel the solitude of the afternoon with her chatty account of her meeting, and how the cake Mrs Dr Gethyn Lewis had brought for the tea had been almost inedible.

'Such a clever woman, but no cook poor thing,' said

Mrs Morgan with ill-concealed satisfaction. She glanced at Sarah curiously. 'Where are the men, then?'

'Gone to Monmouth.'

'Again! What's the reason this time, and why haven't you gone with them?'

Sarah shrugged, trying to look nonchalant. 'In answer to both questions, Mam, I don't know.'

Mrs Morgan obviously considered this odd, but said no more, aware that Sarah wasn't precisely overjoyed about it either, and went off to change. Sarah went back to her garden lounger, but gave up all pretence of reading, and just lay with her face upturned to the sun, telling herself to snap out of her mood. What did she expect? All was now explained, Rupert was innocent as the driven snow in this particular instance, so why did she feel so flat and dissatisfied, she wondered, deciding she was just being unreasonable, and that it might be a good thing to greet Rupert with more warmth when he came back. She heard the latch of the gate and sat up, turning round with a welcoming smile that wavered a little as she saw Rhodri advancing towards her instead of Rupert. He smiled down at her gently.

'Hello.'

'Why hello, Rhodri, I've been meaning to ring you,' she said, flushing. 'Come and sit down.'

Rhodri cast himself down at Sarah's feet on the grass.

'And how's my betrothed?' He smiled up at her, his voice teasing.

Sarah's colour heightened, and her eyes fell. 'I'm afraid the cat's out of the bag, Rhodri,' she confessed, 'and I don't mean your mother's Darius either, although he did rather have a hand in it—or should I say paw.'

Rhodri leaned back on his hands, his face mystified. He shook his head. 'I must be slow on the uptake, or something, Sarah. What's all this about Darius?'

Carefully Sarah gave him a brief outline of the incident and Rupert's subsequent stay at the rectory. 'So despite your chivalrous impulse,' she concluded, 'I'm afraid the parents know our engagement was bogus, and, well—all about Rupert.'

Rhodri was silent for the moment, examining her downcast face.

'I see,' he said slowly. 'So that's it, then, Sarah. God's in his heaven and all that. Are you happy now, love?'

'Oh yes,' she answered brightly. 'I'm just so sorry you have to be involved, and I want you to know I'll always be grateful for your kindness.'

Rhodri winced at that, then glanced up at her thoughtfully. 'It was very enjoyable for me, at least, so let's have no nonsense about kindness. As a matter of interest how do you propose we get disengaged, so to speak?'

Sarah swallowed, feeling worse by the minute. 'Rupert suggests I go back to London and just let things blow over for a while, then you, or I will break off the engagement.'

There was rather a long silence, broken only by the sound of an aeroplane high up in the sky.

'Very organised, your author,' said Rhodri quietly at last. 'You must be the one to do the jilting, Sarah. What possible reason could there be for my wanting to be rid of you?'

She stole a look at him. 'How's your eye?'

'Better. Take a look.' He removed his sunglasses and Sarah gazed directly into his eyes, ignoring the bruise.

'I'm very sorry for, well, for everything, Rhodri.'

He gave her a rueful grin. 'If he doesn't make you happy, tell him I'll beat his brains in.' He rose to his feet and pulled her out of her chair, keeping her hands in his as he smiled down at her flushed face. 'I was just getting used to the role of Sarah Morgan's fiancé, too. Pity really.' He grinned boyishly, lightening the atmosphere. 'If you ever need a shoulder to cry on again, you know where to find me.'

Sarah grinned back, glad to have things straight. 'I'll hold you to that.'

The smile faded from his clear grey eyes as Rhodri stooped and kissed her cheek. 'I'd better be on my way then, Sarah.'

'So soon?' enquired a sarcastic voice, and Sarah looked over Rhodri's shoulder to find Rupert staring at them with murder in his eyes.

Rhodri dropped Sarah's hands and swung round, unperturbed. 'Hello, Clare. I gather apologies are in order.'

Rupert strolled across the grass, one eyebrow raised. 'For which particular offence?' he asked pleasantly.

Sarah could have hit him, and she glanced apprehensively at Rhodri, but the latter merely stood his ground, his jaws clenched as he answered evenly, 'I gather my cat, or rather my mother's, has been the cause of your, er, downfall.'

'It was nothing,' said Rupert tightly, 'my own fault actually.'

'I'm relieved you suffered no serious injury,' said Rhodri courteously, and turned to Sarah. 'Goodbye. No doubt our paths will cross soon again.'

'Goodbye, Rhodri.' She smiled at him warmly.

With a cool nod to Rupert Rhodri took his unhurried departure, stopping for a word with the Rector at the gate, leaving Sarah and Rupert alone together in a hostile, bristling silence broken by Mrs Morgan's arrival.

'Did I catch a glimpse of Rhodri, Sarah?' she asked eagerly.

'He just left.' Sarah avoided Rupert's smouldering look, and stooped to pick up her book.

'Why didn't you offer him a drink?' Mrs Morgan cast bright, inquisitive eyes from one withdrawn face to the other and led them into the house. 'Never mind, let's have a drink in the drawing room, plenty of time before dinner. It's nothing very ambitious I'm afraid, Rupert.'

'I'm sure it will be delicious,' he responded instantly, and turned to greet Sarah's father. 'I'm sorry, sir, I left you to carry the bags.'

Glyn Morgan surrendered the shopping, and sat down, mopping his forehead, while Sarah poured him a glass of sherry.

'Thank you, cariad. Rupert and I have spent quite a

busy time in the town—by the way I tried to persuade Rhodri to join us, but he was in a hurry.'

Rupert smiled sardonically at Sarah as she handed him a glass. 'Only after my appearance on the scene, I imagine.' He raised his glass to her mockingly. 'Two fiancés at a time does seem a little excessive.'

Sarah gave him a furious look, but said nothing, removing herself to a chair as far away as possible from Rupert, while Mrs Morgan stepped hurriedly into the breach.

'Did you find what you wanted in Monmouth, Rupert?'

His smile for her was brilliant with warmth by contrast as he handed her a parcel containing an outsize box of handmade chocolates. 'I did indeed, Mrs Morgan, and I hope you'll like these—I have it on good authority that you possess a secret sweet tooth.'

She was enraptured with her gift, though scolded Rupert when she learned his purchases included two bottles of wine to drink with dinner and another of her husband's favourite brandy.

'You really shouldn't—there was no need——' Mrs Morgan was quite pink with gratitude.

'Just a very small token of appreciation for your hospitality.' Rupert's charm was a potent force, and Elizabeth Morgan responded to it instinctively, as all women did. Sarah looked on with detachment, her eyes narrowing as Rupert came to her and handed over a small gift-wrapped package. She took it reluctantly and looked at it in silence.

'You never let me buy you anything,' he said softly. 'Which is why we left you behind. I wanted a free hand.' He stood over her expectantly, and with her parents watching Sarah had no choice but to remove the paper from a small jeweller's box, to discover a pair of exquisite turquoise and diamond stud earrings on the velvet pad inside. They were a perfect complement to the ring Rupert had had made for her, so she could only assume the gift was some type of declaration of intent. Mrs

Morgan gave a little cry of delight as she came over to peer into the little box, but Sarah merely looked up at Rupert with a polite little smile.

'It's very kind of you, Rupert, but as it happens I already have some turquoise earrings—it's my birthstone, I'm a Sagittarian.' She felt a moment's fleeting satisfaction as his air of expectancy vanished, then remorse gripped her as his eyes grew blank and opaque as he reached out a negligent hand to relieve her of the box.

'No matter, they can easily be exchanged for something else.' He looked at Sarah's parents with a smile. 'Have I time for a quick bath before dinner?'

'Of course, of course, take as long as you like, isn't that right, Beth?' The Rector waved their guest up the stairs, then followed his wife and daughter into the kitchen, closing the door behind him with something suspiciously like a bang. Sarah almost backed away as both parents turned on her in a united front of disapproval.

'Your personal relationships are, of course, your own affair.' Her father's blue eyes were chill. 'Your manners, however, reflect on your parents and your upbringing. You just embarrassed us very much.'

'For shame, Sarah!' Her mother's censure was less remote. 'What a way to behave when Rupert had gone to so much trouble to find such a beautiful present.'

Sarah looked from one to the other miserably, her eyes filling with tears. 'I'm sorry,' she choked, 'but it wasn't a present I wanted.' And with a sob she fled from the kitchen to run upstairs, throwing herself on her bed after taking the precaution of locking her door.

CHAPTER EIGHT

It had been quite unnecessary to lock the door, as no one came to disturb Sarah as she lay on the bed staring at the wall, her tears quickly under control. Half an hour elapsed, during which she heard Rupert moving about in the room next door and eventually going downstairs. When she was sure he was out of the way she got up wearily and went to the bathroom to wash her face before taking off the crumpled sundress, replacing it with the white crêpe-de-chine and putting her pearl drops in her ears rather than cause further offence with the turquoise-studded hoops. She lingered as long as possible over her face and hair before finally nerving herself to go downstairs.

Nerves proved unnecessary. Everyone ignored the incident earlier, and Rupert, elegant in a pintucked white shirt and black linen trousers, was at his most urbane and entertaining in the role of perfect guest, putting Sarah on her mettle. She smiled and contributed to the conversation with vivacity while they ate melon served with curls of wafer-thin ham, followed by crisply grilled trout flanked by French beans with almonds and tiny new potatoes. Sarah insisted that her mother remain seated while she herself removed plates and brought in fruit and cheese. Rupert watched her inscrutably as she flitted to and fro, his smile sardonic when she sent him a glittering look across the table as she seated herself in a flurry of pleats just as the telephone rang. The Rector got up and laid down his napkin, excusing himself, only to return almost at once.

'For you, Sarah,' he said, looking a trifle uncomfortable. 'Rhodri.'

Sarah avoided Rupert's eye, and left the room with an apology to cross the hall to her father's study.

'Hello,' she said cautiously.

'Sarah, I hope I'm not disturbing you, but I felt I had to ring to see if you were all right. I couldn't help feeling concerned—my presence this afternoon obviously made things awkward.'

'No, not in the least,' she answered untruthfully. 'But thank you for worrying about me.'

'I'm going back to London in the morning.' He hesitated a moment. 'Look, Sarah, I thought you might like my address and telephone number in London.'

'Why thank you—I'll scribble it down, right got it, Rhodri.'

'You might like to give me a ring if you're in need of a chat, or something,' he said lightly.

'That's very sweet of you.' Sarah was touched. 'By the way, I still have the ring.'

'I'd like to make a grandiose gesture and tell you to keep it as a memento,' he chuckled, 'but it's one of my mother's—and I don't think your author would be very pleased, either.'

'You're so right! I'll send it to you by registered post.'

'Thanks, Sarah. Take care. Goodbye.'

'The thanks are all on my side, Rhodri. Goodbye.'

Sarah put the phone down and stood staring at it abstractedly. Suddenly a hand reached in front of her and tore off the top page of her father's memo-pad, where Rhodri's address was scribbled. She whirled round to glare into Rupert's cold eyes.

'You were eavesdropping!' she accused him hotly.

'You bet your sweet life I was, sweetheart,' he drawled, and crumpled the paper into a ball. Very illuminating, too—everything all ironed out now?'

'Oh yes.' Sarah's eyes flashed blue fire as she stared defiantly at him. 'Rhodri sent you a message this afternoon, by the way. I forgot to relay it.'

'Did he indeed!'

'He said that if you don't make me happy he'll bash your brains in.'

'Belligerent little chap!' Rupert's nostrils flared and his

eyes took on an angry glitter that made Sarah back away instinctively.

'We'd better get back to the table,' she said huskily, suddenly afraid, his grip hurting her wrist. Rupert dropped her hand and motioned her through the door.

They both made a pretence of eating dessert, but when bidden to sit in the drawing room for coffee by Mrs Morgan, Rupert flashed his white smile at her and confided he was so replete with all the delicious food he felt in need of exercise.

'Would you mind if I took Sarah for a walk?' he asked, indicating the sunset beyond the windows. 'It's such a perfect evening it seems a shame to spend it indoors. Perhaps you both might care to join us?'

'But I should help wash up——' began Sarah.

'No, no.' The Rector shook his head. 'I'll give your mother a hand, you're excused for this evening. You can have your coffee and brandy when you get back.'

A walk alone with Rupert was the last thing Sarah wanted at this particular moment, but she went obediently up to her room to search for an old pair of flat white sandals, reflecting grimly that an evening of polite four-handed conversation with her parents was by no means a tempting alternative either. On the whole it would be better to go out and get their differences settled, as something in Rupert's manner suggested a volcano on the point of eruption, and from past experience she would prefer him to do any erupting as far from the rectory as possible.

Sarah led Rupert through the back garden and the orchard into the serene little churchyard and through the lychgate, some perverse instinct making her choose the narrow, steep footpath where she and Rhodri had walked only a few days earlier. Her ominously silent companion followed her closely as Sarah went ahead up the narrow, overgrown track, until he pulled her unceremoniously back, going in front of her to hold back the brambles and straying branches. Rupert's pace was deliberately punishing once he led the way, forging ahead at a rate she found hard to match, and by the time they reached the stone stile leading to the open ground at the top Sarah's heart was thumping and she was breathless.

'Could we have a breather, Rupert?' she gasped. He plucked her over and set her down on her feet like a sack of potatoes.

'If you want.' His breathing seemed quite normal as he glanced down at her with impersonal curiosity. 'You seem smaller.'

'Only because I've changed my shoes.' Sarah breathed deeply as she turned to look at the sun, which was making a theatrically beautiful exit over the rolling hills beyond them. Rupert watched it with her while her breathing slowed, making no attempt to break the silence all the time they watched the dramatic colours fade to leave the stage for the appearance of the first star.

'Recovered?' he asked after a while. Sarah nodded and they set off at a more leisurely pace up the last slope, then down again over the sheep-cropped turf, skirting outcroppings of rock here and there. They passed the spot where she and Rhodri had rested, continuing for some distance until they reached a dingle with a close-clustering copse of trees. Rupert stopped abruptly in a small clearing in the heart of the copse and stripped off his black cashmere sweater, throwing it down on the grass.

'Let's sit awhile,' he said brusquely. It was an order, not a suggestion, and Sarah sat obediently. He threw himself down alongside her and lay propped on one elbow. 'Why did Lloyd-Ellis give you his address?' he asked harshly.

'He thought I might need it some time.' Sarah hugged her arms round her knees and peered uneasily through the trees surrounding them. The utter stillness made her nervous. They might have been the only two people in the world.

'Why the hell should you be likely to do that?' Rupert's voice grated in the quiet.

'I don't know. Maybe he has doubts about my chance of happiness with you.' Sarah cast a defiant glance at his

face, but he was half-turned away from her, and the
rapidly fading light hid Rupert's expression.

'Do you?' he asked flatly.

'I didn't say that.'

'You didn't need to.' He turned towards her. 'Why did
you throw the earrings back in my face this afternoon,
Sarah?'

'I didn't.'

'As good as.'

'They were obviously meant to match the ring, and it
all seemed so matter-of-fact and taken for granted, as
though you were smugly sure of me once I'd heard your
side of the story, without, well, without any other sort of
assurances.' She recoiled as he leant forward, his
brooding face close to hers.

'There was no "side", just the truth,' he said forcefully,
'and for your information the earrings were intended as a
tribute, a pledge—oh, what the hell! They obviously
didn't mean the same to you.'

'No, they didn't. I would have liked matters made a
little clearer on your part first, that's all.'

'And there was I, like a romantic fool, thinking I was
making it clear in the best way possible.' At the sneer in
his voice Sarah shrank farther away. 'Don't worry,' he
said bitterly. 'I'm not going to hurt you.'

'I didn't think you were,' said Sarah with dignity.

'Tell me one thing, Sarah, truthfully, if you can
manage it. Do you have a slight, lingering feeling that
your gallant Celt would be a better proposition than me?'

'Yes, I do,' she said baldly.

Rupert flung away from her, presenting a view of his
shoulders, the white of his shirt glimmering through the
dusk.

'So your—feeling for me was a delicate little plant,' he
muttered. 'It perished at the first touch of frost.'

'How poetic, Rupert!'

'Words are my trade.'

'And you did ask for the truth,' she reminded him. 'I
answered your question honestly, as you asked. You did

say a slight, lingering feeling, after all. I've known Rhodri all my life—he wasn't some casual pick-up on a train, and surely it's only natural if I do feel a slight tinge of regret.'

'All right, all right, spare me chapter and verse,' he said testily.

'It's impossible to have a reasonable conversation with you,' snapped Sarah, offended.

Rupert drew closer. 'All I brought you out here to learn Sarah, is whether you still want me as a husband.'

His voice was harsh and Sarah stared at him wordlessly, trying to read the expression in his eyes, desperately needing some evidence of tenderness, some small demonstration of the love Rupert had never put into words, but he loomed close, his body tense, making no attempt to touch her and the silence went on a fraction too long.

'I see,' he said at last conversationally. 'Perhaps I should help you make up your mind.'

Sarah tensed, her mouth suddenly dry as she backed away in scrambling, ungraceful haste across the grass, gathering herself to spring to her feet and run, but Rupert was before her, pushing her flat with an insultingly casual hand, then knocking all the breath out of her as his body came down on top of her. She twisted her head from side to side in futile protest, her mouth opening to gasp in air. He laughed deep in his throat and caught one of her flailing hands in his, holding it behind her head until he captured the other, holding both hands in his while his mouth descended on hers to smother her furious demands for freedom. The kiss continued as a punitive measure that finally achieved its aim. Sarah lay limp at last, overcome by sheer superior strength. He slid his arms round her, holding her cruelly tight as he lifted his head just enough to look down into her enraged eyes as she fought for breath.

'I have had you in my house, within my reach day after day,' he said with ominous quiet, 'and I have kept docilely at arm's length, tamely accepting any meagre crumbs of love you allowed me. And my reward was to watch you at that wedding, paraded as another man's property, when all the time you belonged to me.' He laughed in self-derision. 'I was so virtuous, so biddable. Not once did I try to coax you across the threshold of my bedroom.'

'Which was just as well,' spat Sarah breathlessly. 'The only time I did cross it there was another woman in the bed!'

Rupert's hands bit cruelly into her flesh. 'I've explained all that, woman!'

'Don't call me woman!'

'I grant you it's a debatable description.'

They glared into each other's eyes like sworn enemies, their breath coming in painful gasps, Sarah's half from his weight and half from fear, Rupert's not only from rage, but from the effect of another emotion that was obviously beginning to dominate him to the exclusion of all others.

'Well?' he demanded roughly.

'Well what?' she panted. 'What do you want me to say?'

'I want you to say yes!'

'To what?' Sarah's voice cracked in desperation.

'To me, and only to me. To marriage and commitment, Sarah!'

At any other time, and in any other place her response would have been in the affirmative, and gladly. But crushed beneath his weight, virtually bludgeoned into answering, Sarah turned obstinate, some last shreds of independence turning her head to one side in silent negation, a last burst of defiance. But the defiance flamed into raw fear as she felt his whole body grow taut, like a predator about to spring, then there was no thought or emotion left in her but the burning need for defence and opposition. Wildly she twisted and struggled against hands that were alternatively rough and persuasive, and a mouth that possessed and punished, allowing her to gulp in air only when his lips raised a fraction to slide down her throat, his tongue searing a path as he licked at the salty taste of her fear. At this she grew frantic as he restrained her wrists again in one cruel hand while the other removed her clothes so swiftly she hardly realised she was nude until his own body covered hers, as bare as her own. Sarah abandoned all pretence of dignity. She babbled hoarse entreaties even as she fought, but Rupert was blind and deaf to anything but the primitive urge to subdue and possess.

At one stage his efforts to hold her down metamorphosed into caresses intended to inflame, but Sarah was conscious only of indignities and sensations never experienced before, by far the worst part her own utter helplessness to withstand the lips, the tongue, the diabolical fingers that made her writhe and pant as he finally dispelled her certainty that she was a separate entity, as for the first time she became an interdependent component of a rhythmic process that went on in an inexorable progression towards some unknown goal that the man above her reached alone with a hoarse cry of triumph, leaving her deflated and desolate, with a shattering feeling of loss.

Where everything had been all chaos and struggle, now it was preternaturally still, except for the slowing breathing of the body that still held her pinned, like some primitive sacrifice, to the earth. Sarah felt the air cold on the sweat that encased her body in a slick film. She opened her eyes dully to find the rising moon illuminating the scene with the sudden brilliance of a light switched on in a darkened room. She blinked and turned her head away from the thick, wild hair of the head that lay like a weight on her breast.

'Have you finished?' she asked, with a precise clarity that rocketed Rupert to his feet to pull on his clothes rapidly, Sarah too apathetic to make the effort to get up and search for her own. Rupert stood over her, and she shuddered with revulsion, averting her eyes from the sight of him staring down at her. Abruptly he turned away and collected her scattered garments, handing them to her without a word.

'Please turn your back,' she said evenly.

'Isn't it a bit late for that?' he asked huskily.

'Suit yourself.' Sarah got up indifferently and dressed herself with difficulty, too numb to care whether he watched or not. She was slow and unco-ordinated, her fingers clumsy, and her movements awkward. With belated delicacy Rupert left her alone to struggle on as best she could, standing still and watchful as she finally managed to slide home the zip at the back of her dress. He held out his hand.

'Ready? Let's go back.'

Sarah stood looking at his outstretched hand with dislike.

'If it is at all possible,' she said deliberately, 'I would prefer not to come into physical contact with you ever again.' She turned her back on him, threading her way swiftly through the copse before climbing doggedly up the slopes beyond it, ignoring the soreness and aches in various parts of her body, all her energies channelled into just getting home, to crawl into bed and hide. Sarah climbed over the stile at the top before Rupert could offer assistance, and descended the overhung path at a punishing rate that proved her undoing. She tripped on a root in the darkness, toppling on her hands and knees in an inelegant sprawl. Instantly Rupert raised her to her feet, then dropped his hands, moving away before she could push him.

'Are you hurt, Sarah?'

'Only my dignity.' She resumed the descent with more caution, thankful when they finally arrived at the kitchen door of the rectory. She felt thirsty and utterly exhausted, and grateful beyond words that her parents had gone to bed. In the cruelly bright light of the kitchen Rupert and Sarah looked at each other for a moment. Her main reaction was one of gratitude for the fact that no one was there to see the spectacle they presented. Rupert's shirt was torn and the partly healed scratches on his face had opened slightly, a trickle of blood issuing from the deepest. Sarah knew her hair was a tangled mess, her lips felt swollen, and there was a graze on one leg where she'd fallen, apart from bruises that were already making themselves felt on various regions of her body hidden by her clothes. Rupert made a move towards her, his face urgent.

'Sarah——'

She held up a hand, retreating instinctively. 'Please. Don't say anything.'

His eyes darkened. 'Sarah, we *must* talk. Surely you can see——'

'There's nothing to discuss,' she interrupted quickly. Her eyes fell on the coffee-tray left for them. 'May I offer you some coffee?'

'I don't *want* any bloody coffee!' Rupert's fists clenched as he glared at her, frustrated.

'Oh. Well in that case I may as well go to bed. Goodnight.'

Sarah left him and went upstairs to shut herself into the bathroom. At least if her mother heard her the fall would provide a good excuse for her second bath in only a few hours. She allowed herself only a short time in the hot water, wincing at the sting of it on her protesting flesh as she lathered herself all over, scrubbing fiercely in an attempt to remove all traces of Rupert's attentions. She sluiced cold water over herself afterwards until she was gasping and breathless, then stole back to her bedroom huddled in a towelling robe. Sarah stood at her open window for a long time in the darkness, indifferent to the cool air playing on her wet hair. After her energetic scrubbing her body felt a little better, but her depression and resentment deepened as she realised that nothing similar was likely to expunge the evening's experience from her mind. Rupert had gone berserk. She found it hard to credit that he could have burst through the barrier of her inexperience with such a lack of sensitivity. Whatever happened to Rupert Clare the great lover? If that was a sample of his expertise all those other women must have been deranged.

Sarah was still at her post as the clock struck one. The

house was quiet, everyone presumably asleep, but she went on standing there until a burning thirst sent her silently out of the room and down the stairs. She closed the kitchen door behind her and made for the refrigerator without turning on the light. She took out an ice-tray and dropped several cubes into a glass before filling it with water from the tap, gulping the cold liquid down thirstily at the sink, spluttering suddenly as two hands gripped her waist from behind. She whirled round to confront Rupert in the darkness.

'What are you doing here? Are you mad?' The hostility in her whisper fairly crackled as she glared up into the darkness of his unseen face above the just-visible glimmer of his white shirt.

'I couldn't sleep, so I thought I'd take a walk in the garden, but then I heard you leave your room. I had to talk to you, Sarah.' His hand came up to touch her shoulder, but she shrugged it away immediately.

'There's nothing you can say.' Her voice was quiet and bitter. 'Your actions tonight spoke louder than all the thousands of words you've ever dictated to me.'

'Sarah, listen to me.' Rupert's voice sounded strained, disembodied, but Sarah turned her back on him unmoved. He came closer, and with the sink in front of her there was no way she could avoid him. His breath was warm on the back of her neck as he spoke with impassioned urgency in her ear. 'When I saw Lloyd-Ellis kissing you in the garden this afternoon it was only a sense of courtesy to your parents that kept me from punching him in the nose. Then afterwards you were so distant and detached, turning up your nose at my present, and finally there was a note in your voice that scared the hell out of me when you were talking on the phone to the same blasted man. All I could think of was that you were mine, and somehow I had to make you realise it, admit it. I—I went too far, right over the top, I know, and I'd give much to undo it, but please try to understand the instinct that motivated me.'

'Oh I do.' Sarah took a deep breath. 'Your motivation

was painfully obvious. What I find hard to forgive is the—the way you went about it. If that wasn't rape it was the next best thing, and if that's what makes the world go round I'm glad I hung on to my amateur status as long as I did. If that's love, or rather sex, I'd rather go a few rounds with a heavy-weight boxer.' She felt him wince, fiercely glad that her barbs had found their mark.

'It needn't have been like that,' he said hoarsely. 'You fought like a wildcat.'

'What did you expect?' She twisted round suddenly, her face turned up to his in the darkness. 'Why did you do such a thing?'

'Some primitive idea of putting my mark on you, I suppose. I suspected, hoped——'

'That I was pure and innocent!'

'Precisely. When you wouldn't say yes out there in the wood I lost my head. I suppose I thought, or felt, that if I possessed you physically and I was the first one to do so, you would naturally——'

'Lick your boots if you made an honest woman of me?' The venom in Sarah's quiet voice acted on Rupert like a goad, and he stood with teeth clenched as the soft, upbraiding voice continued. 'This is the twentieth century, Rupert. You spend so much time steeped in the past you've let it take over your attitude towards me. I'm not the deflowered heroine of one of your medieval sagas, Rupert Clare. I don't need the protection of your celebrated name just because you were the first past the post.'

Rupert drew a deep, unsteady breath, obviously fighting to stay calm.

'I've explained my reasons, Sarah. I can't undo what happened, so for God's sake stop carrying on like a tragedy queen and bow to the inevitable.' He jerked her into his arms and kissed her, his patience exhausted. Sarah endured his embrace with tightly shut mouth, her body rigid and unyielding, until Rupert's arms fell slowly away and he stepped back. 'That's it, then,' he said.

'Goodnight, Sarah. My deepest apologies once again for my earlier behaviour. It won't happen again.'

'You're dead right about that.' Sarah stood belligerently, her arms folded across her chest. For a time they stood in hostile silence in the dark, then to Sarah's fury she heard Rupert yawn. Once again he bade her goodnight, this time with the utmost formality, and left the room quietly, leaving her frustrated and affronted, hardly knowing what she had expected, but certainly something more than his abrupt departure. She knew Rupert too well to imagine him on his knees in supplication, but some quirk of perversity had expected something more persuasive in the way of repentance.

After a while Sarah went drearily upstairs and climbed into bed, her body clamouring for sleep but her mind so active that the first faint glow of dawn was in the sky before she dozed off. It was late when she woke, and guiltily she washed and dressed at speed before running down to the kitchen to find her mother at the table with a cup of coffee and the morning paper, and no one else in sight.

'Sorry, Mam,' she said breathlessly. 'I overslept.'

Mrs Morgan smiled cheerfully and laid down the paper. 'You must have been tired love. I wanted to give you a call, but Rupert wouldn't let me disturb you.'

Sarah frowned. 'Rupert? Is he up already, then?'

'Why yes, love. Apparently he wanted to get an early start.' Mrs Morgan stared at Sarah's blank face. 'He left before nine, darling. He was going to take the Metro back, then make straight for London, remember?'

'Yes, of course,' said Sarah abstractedly. 'I just didn't realise he was leaving quite so soon.' Which was the literal truth. She sat down abruptly. 'Any coffee in the pot, Mother?'

'Yes, plenty. Something to eat?'

Sarah shook her head. 'No, I don't think so, thanks.' She hesitated as her mother poured coffee into a mug for her. 'Did he leave a message for me?'

Mrs Morgan nodded, smiling. 'There's a note for you

on the desk in the study. Your father's gone over to Llanhowell today for lunch with the Rev Beynon there, so it's just the two of us until Mari-Siân comes home.'

'I'll take my coffee into the study then,' said Sarah and went to look for Rupert's note. She sat at her father's desk for some time looking at the envelope on the blotter. It was addressed simply to 'Sarah' in Rupert's angular script, and she felt reluctant to open it, finishing her coffee before taking the single sheet of paper from the envelope with unsteady fingers. There was no greeting.

'I spent the night taking stock of our relationship, Sarah. I came to several conclusions. First, I can never hope to be the "parfait gentil knight" you seem to require. I try, but nothing seems to go to plan. With regard to the incident with Naomi I plead innocence, though for last night's crime I can only plead guilty, with extenuating circumstances. After much thought, little dragon, I don't feel I can face a life where I land in the dock every so often. Particularly when it seems I can only expect prosecution, never defence. Frankly, that's not a viable way of life. At least not as I see it. I can't undo last night. I would if I could, but I can at least leave the field for your tame Celt. He's not the type to step out of line. Don't misunderstand. My feelings towards you are unchanged. I just can't live up to you. Mea culpa, Sarah. Try to forgive me. Say nothing to your parents for the time being if it makes things easier for you. Please keep the ring. It was made for you, after all. I only wish I was.

R.'

Sarah gazed blankly at the ring lying on the desk top, the bottom fallen out of her world. Idly she swung to and fro in her father's swivel chair her eyes fixed on Rupert's handwriting, almost as if she expected the meaning to change if she waited long enough. The truth was unpalatable but Sarah looked it square in the face, admitting that she had received her just desserts. Yesterday she had been capricious and petty, viewed in retrospect, puffed up with the conceit of having two males in tow. Her aim had been to make Rupert suffer a little, show him that he wasn't the only one with other strings to his bow before she graciously bestowed her hand, but her plan had misfired badly. She laughed mirthlessly at a mental picture of both Rupert and Rhodri speeding along the M4 to London neck and neck, leaving her with two expensive, meaningless rings for company.

She did her best to be dispassionate as she went over Rupert's jerky, uncharacteristic sentences, nothing like the flowing vigour of the prose that was his literary trademark. He was right of course. Once aware of the heady potency of her own physical attraction for Rupert, and something of the unexpected power it gave her, Sarah had dictated all the moves in their game of love with the arrogance of a female dictator. And now, she thought bitterly, she had her come-uppance. Checkmate.

CHAPTER NINE

In comparison with the journey down to Newport Sarah's return to London was dull in the extreme. With no tall, good-looking fellow-traveller as diversion Sarah's thoughts were depressing companions. The time since Rupert's abrupt departure had gone by like years instead of weeks. At first Sarah could hardly bring herself to believe he really meant to disappear out of her life. She existed in a constant, frustrated state of expectancy, hoping every telephone call was Rupert ringing her to say it was all a mistake. But he never rang at all, which was not only shattering to Sarah, but embarrassing. She took to staying up very late so that she could tell her parents about imaginary calls Rupert made to her at night, when everyone was in bed. She found the effort of hiding her misery exhausting, and longed to confide in her parents, but something had happened which had put this out of the question.

On a trip to Monmouth one day Glyn Morgan learned from one of his parishioners that Mari-Sîan had been present at an all-night party in the town when she was supposed to be spending the night with her friend, Bronwen Parry, who had told *her* mother she was staying the night at the rectory. Glyn Morgan was in a truly towering rage when he found out, all forbearance for once swept away by anger. His child's deceit was the matter that concerned him, much more than the fact that the party concerned was rather rowdy and a cause for complaint from people in the neighbourhood. There was a thoroughly horrifying scene with the Rector and Mrs Morgan angry and hurt, Mari-Sîan defiant and tearful, and Sarah trying in vain to act as mediator. The row culminated in Glyn Morgan's collapse with pains in his chest, which terrified Mari-Sîan, sent his wife running for his pills and Sarah to the telephone for the doctor.

In a short while Glyn Morgan was well again, but it was a salutary experience for Sarah. The news of her break with Rupert, not to mention her lack of a job, would have to wait indefinitely. Sarah refused to endanger her father's health by giving him any more shocks if she could help it. A few days later Rhia and Charles came back from their honeymoon, laden with presents, to spend a few hours at the rectory before going on to Gareth's to collect Kate and Emma. Rhia was so radiant her presence acted like a tonic on her father, and Sarah was able to leave home the following Sunday with no qualms about his health to add to her other problems.

Sarah's tiny flat seemed airless and lacking in welcome when she let herself in. The summer evening was warm, and the city pavements claustrophobic after the green countryside of home. Trying to shrug off her depression Sarah unpacked, setting Rhia's glass goblet from Murano on her small television where she could look at its warm honey colour and satisfying shape whenever the programme on the set was boring. Rhia had given it to her with a kiss, teasing Sarah unmercifully when she heard of the bogus 'betrothal' and Rupert's subsequent resumption of Rhodri's role of fiancé, with lots of laughing references to 'dark horses' and 'safety in numbers'. The former barrier between Rhia and Sarah was gone for good, whatever lingering remnants there might have been swept away by the radiant creature so happy in her marriage she wanted everyone to share her joy.

Sarah grudged her none of it. Nevertheless there was a new life to plan for herself. In bed in the flat that night Sarah faced the future without flinching. She was now one of the ranks of the unemployed, and tomorrow she would go along to the DHSS, and from there to the Agency and throw herself on Miss Frobisher's mercy if she were still in charge. Sarah's eyes strayed to the telephone on her bedside table. It would be so easy to pick it up and dial Rupert's number, but she dismissed that idea at once, unable to face the thought of more rejection.

She had sent back the sapphire ring to Rhodri, and received a friendly note in return, but Rupert's ring lay in an inner zipped pocket of her handbag now she was away from home. It had been an agony to wear it, knowing that it was just an empty sham, and she was glad to hide it away.

Sarah got up to wander round the flat restlessly, unable to sleep, wondering why she couldn't have been sensible enough to fall in love with Rhodri Lloyd-Ellis. God knows he was attractive and eligible enough, and would certainly never have subjected her to a crude, uncaring assault like Rupert's. It would be utterly uncharacteristic. Sarah stopped her pacing, struck by the thought that it was uncharacteristic of Rupert too, now she considered it impartially. All his pursuits of women had been deliberate, suavely executed affairs, with the recipients of his attentions positively ga-ga with bliss, if the subsequent lamentations were anything to go by once his interest was diverted elsewhere. So why should *she* get unlucky, thought Sarah with resentment, still smarting at the memory of Rupert's treatment. Deciding she was just the unlucky type, Sarah went back to bed, determined to get a good night's rest before facing the rigours of Monday and the harsh reality of searching for a job.

Miss Frobisher was still in charge at the Agency, to Sarah's relief, and briskly promised to do her best, though proved pessimistic about anything immediate. It was a forlorn Sarah who returned to her flat. If a job wasn't forthcoming fairly shortly eating was likely to become a luxury. Her finances were dwindling rapidly, and although she still had a roof over her head for the time being the outlook was bleak. It was funny in one way to think that Rupert still owed her a month's salary, though she would rather starve than ask him for it.

During the following week Sarah answered several advertisements and filled in numerous application forms, her depression deepening with every passing day. Then towards the end of the week she was invited to two interviews. One was with an exporting firm who demanded German, not French, the other with a small firm of solicitors who offered Sarah the job on the spot, to her utter relief. Only one small point marred her jubilation. Not unnaturally they required a reference from Rupert, and Sarah supplied the necessary address, thankful it was late on a Friday, and she would have a chance to ring Rupert and ask him first, before Messrs Blenkinsop and Pringle contacted him after the weekend.

Sarah spent all that evening ringing Rupert's number, without any success. Each time she let the phone ring until she nearly went mad, and finally was obliged to go to bed miserable, wondering where he was and who he was with. Her luck was no better next day, which developed into a waking nightmare, with nowhere to go and no one to talk to. Don McFarlane, the attractive young accountant in the flat below had moved, his place taken by an earnest young woman who posted CND stickers in the hall, and the rest of the building was occupied by young couples who were friendly when Sarah met them in passing, but had their own lives to live. Loneliness and worry smudged dark marks beneath Sarah's eyes, and she cursed the day she'd set eyes on Rupert Clare. In one fell swoop he'd neatly deprived her of everything, a deeply interesting job, her love, even her 'long preserved virginity'.

The following morning Sarah was made hideously aware of yet another of Rupert's achievements. When she got out of bed she had to bolt to the bathroom to be sick. Coughing and gasping miserably she stared into the mirror, doing a hasty bit of arithmetic and failing to come up with the right answer. There was no point in blaming the takeaway curry consumed listlessly the evening before. Sarah sank down on the edge of the bath, her legs trembling, and tried to come to terms with this new, unthinkable development. It was beyond her. At the prospect of being pregnant a great swamping tide of panic rose inside Sarah, and she crumpled into a heap on the tiled floor, her head in her arms, and sobbed with bitter abandon. It was some time before she could even bring herself to get up from the floor and wash and dress herself. A plain biscuit and a hot cup of tea restored her to something fairly like calm, and she even managed a faint grin at the thought that her predecessor had left Rupert because she was pregnant, too, only she had been respectably married, lucky lady.

Trying to think sensibly she came to the conclusion that for the time being she would just have to take the job at Blenkinsop and Pringle, to give her a bit of financial backing, that reminded her that there was still the matter of the reference to sort out. With unsteady fingers she dialled Rupert's number for what seemed like the fiftieth time, but with no luck, wondering dismally if he had changed it just so that she wouldn't be able to contact him. Sarah's eyes hardened. She would go round to St John's Wood and ring his doorbell. Just like all those others, a small voice sneered. Sarah ignored it. If no one was in the house she could use her own key and leave Rupert a note, asking for the most glowing reference he could manage, then she would leave the key behind and there would be no need to have anything to do with Rupert Clare ever again. This sensible thought made Sarah so unhappy she felt sick again, which delayed her departure until she felt sufficiently fit to negotiate the Underground.

When Sarah arrived in Hamilton Terrace she rang the doorbell of Rupert's lovely house three times before concluding that no one was likely to answer it. Deciding Mrs Dobson must also be away she let herself in, feeling as guilty as a criminal as she tiptoed furtively across the hall. Sarah put her head round the kitchen door but the big room was empty and vaguely unkempt. No Mrs Dobson, obviously. The silence was oppressive, and Sarah felt nervous as she opened the study door and crossed to the table to scribble a note. As she sat down Sarah cast a look around the room where she had spent so much of her time over the past few years, then with a sigh she took a pen from the stand, giving a shriek of pure terror as a hand closed on her shoulder and she was yanked out of her seat up against a bare chest to stare in speechless shock at Rupert's malevolent, unshaven face.

'Breaking and entering, by God,' he said in a slurred, thickened voice. 'Who'd have thought it of the parson's daughter?'

'Rupert!' Sarah felt ill with fright, her breath coming in painful gasps.

'Who the hell did you expect? I live here. Or had it slipped your mind already?' He glowered down at her with bloodshot eyes, the stale smell of alcohol wrinkling Sarah's nose with disgust.

'You're drunk—and at this time of the morning!' Her look of frigid distaste stirred some chord of angry response in him and his fingers tightened on her arms.

'That's the girl—always the kind word. Got to hand it to you, Sarah, you're bloody c-consistent.' His teeth bared in a travesty of a smile, then he winced and put a hand to his forehead. 'God, my head!'

'Hangover,' said Sarah without sympathy, and rubbed her shoulder, which already felt bruised. She surveyed him without pleasure. The charismatic Mr Clare was hardly likely to quicken any female heartbeats in his present condition. Barefoot, wearing only a pair of familiar track-suit trousers, his chin dark with several days growth of beard and hair badly in need of cutting, he looked like some desperado on the run. He stood, swaying slightly, returning her scrutiny with interest.

'You look a bit the worse for wear, Sarah,' he said, to her intense annoyance.

'Coming from you that's a laugh.' Her eyes flashed blue fire, but not enough to divert his attention from the tell-tale marks beneath them. He shook his head solemnly.

'Not sh-sleeping well by the look of you. Lloyd-Ellis keeping you out of your bed at night—or perhaps he's keeping you *in* it!'

'Don't be disgusting,' she snapped. 'Apart from which it can hardly be of interest to you.'

'I wouldn't say that.' Rupert tilted his head to one

side, eyeing her with curiosity. 'What were you after in the study, anyway?'

Sarah looked away. 'I was leaving you a note asking you to give me an extravagantly good reference. I start work with a firm of solicitors next week. I've tried and tried to reach you on the telephone but as there was no answer I finally resorted to using my key. You'd better have it back.' She thrust it into his hand. 'I thought Mrs Dobson would have answered the phone, at least.'

Rupert stood looking owlishly at the keyring, not seeming to take in what she was saying. He looked up vaguely. 'She's not here. I would have answered, but I switched off my bedroom extension and I can't hear this one up there.'

'I see.' Sarah looked at him thoughtfully. 'Where's Mrs Dobson?'

'She kept bothering me about meals, so I told her to take some time off.'

'When did you eat last?'

Rupert shrugged indifferently. 'No idea.'

Sarah lost patience. 'How idiotic!'

'Sticks and stones may break my bones,' he chanted, the look in his eyes chilling Sarah. They were blank and green as glass.

'Why are you drinking like this, Rupert?' she asked, frowning.

'Why d'you think, little dragon? Because I'm thirsty!' His meaningless grin grew fixed, the empty eyes suddenly filling with consternation. 'Do excuse me,' he murmured politely, and made a dive for the cloakroom, where it was impossible to ignore the fact that Rupert Clare was being violently sick.

Must be contagious, thought Sarah wryly, and went to the kitchen. Mrs Dobson's immaculately kept cupboards were full of tins and packaged groceries, including fresh coffee beans, but the refrigerator held only a few bottles of tonic-water, a piece of elderly cheese and a bowl of eggs. Sarah found some bread in the freezer and put the loaf to thaw while she opened a tin of French onion soup filled the percolator and located a tin of powdered milk. A wan, hollow-eyed apparition finally appeared in the doorway.

'Thought you'd gone,' said Rupert morosely.

'As you don't seemed disposed to use the sense you were born with, I thought I'd better get some solid nourishment inside you to mop up the excess of liquid variety.' Sarah smiled with malice as he shuddered at the prospect. Rupert looked down at himself with distaste, and ran a hand over the villainous stubble on his chin.

'If I go and clean up will you hang on until I get down?' he asked, with a touch of something almost like diffidence.

'Yes. If you promise to eat what I put in front of you.'

Rupert agreed without enthusiasm, and retreated up the curve of the staircase in the direction of his room.

Sarah sank down on one of the kitchen chairs, her mind working at a tremendous rate. If Rupert was drowning his sorrows in drink, was she over-optimistic to hope that the reason for his misery was her own absence? The thought was immensely cheering and Sarah finished the preparations for the snack meal in a very much improved state of mind. By the time Rupert came down the scent of freshly percolated coffee was in the air, the soup was bubbling appetisingly, and with some difficulty she had managed to hack a few slices of bread from the semi-thawed loaf with the electric knife.

It was hard to associate the unkempt ruffian of shortly before with the closely shaven, haggardly elegant creature who reappeared in his place. His immaculate beige linen shirt and trousers made Sarah feel suddenly dowdy in her plain blue cotton dress as he smiled at her with grave apology, a greyish cast to his brown skin.

'Forgive my unspeakable appearance when you arrived, Sarah. I wasn't expecting company.'

'Think nothing of it.' Sarah put a cup of coffee in front of him as he sat down at the table. Rupert sipped the hot liquid with caution, and there was an awkward silence.

'Will you have some soup?' asked Sarah brightly. 'Out

of a tin, I'm afraid, but there's some grated cheese, and I've made some toast to eat with it.'

'How resourceful. Thank you.'

The strained atmosphere was beginning to tell on Sarah. She put a bowl of soup in front of him and picked up her handbag, deciding enough was enough.

'Aren't you joining me Sarah?' His eyes held hers steadily, as a slight flush crept into her cheeks.

'I hadn't thought——'

'Please. Don't condemn me to a solitary meal.'

'Thank you.'

She filled a bowl for herself, accepted some grated cheese from the plate he offered, and they both began to eat in silence. To her gratification Rupert's bowl emptied at top speed, and Sarah rose automatically to refill it, but he waved her back and served himself.

'Half an hour or so ago I wouldn't have believed it possible to look soup in the face, let alone enjoy it,' observed Rupert with surprise.

'I chose this flavour because I believe that's how the recipe originated.' Sarah ventured a smile at him. 'Concocted by French housewives as a restorative for the master of the house when—well, under the same circumstances.'

'Stoned out of his mind, you mean.' He gave her a grin that lightened the atmosphere a little.

'Your description, not mine!' Sarah got to her feet, feeling considerably better herself. 'Could you eat some more?'

Rupert looked a little shamefaced. 'Strangely enough I still feel hungry,' he admitted, 'but I fancy something a little more solid than soup.'

'There are tins galore, but otherwise I can only find eggs.' Sarah raised an eyebrow. 'An omelette, perhaps?'

'If it's not putting you to too much trouble, Sarah.' There was a grave formality in Rupert's voice that saddened Sarah a little. She preferred him rude and hungover to this withdrawn courtesy.

'Not at all.' She took her tone from him and went over

to the ceramic hobbs let into one of the counter tops. She took down an omelette pan from a row of them hanging on the wall. Within minutes a fluffy, perfect omelette was folded on to a warm plate and set in front of the man watching her perform her culinary magic in silence.

'I didn't know you could cook,' he said expressionlessly.

'You never asked.' Sarah poured herself some coffee and sat down again, watching him polish off the omelette and several slices of thick bread before he sat back, obviously feeling, and looking, a lot better.

'Thank you, Sarah. That was just what I needed.'

'Coffee?'

'Please.'

With the idea of preventing that stifling silence Sarah said, 'I started ringing you a couple of days ago, Rupert. Have you been, well, under the weather *all* the time?'

'More or less.' He leaned back in his chair, watching her quick, efficient movements. 'You could put those in the dishwasher—though it's probably full. I've just gone on loading it since Mrs Dobson left.'

Sarah opened the dishwasher gingerly and viewed its contents with a grin.

'I see what you mean. I'll just add these things and do the lot, then. Have you been away?' she added casually.

'Yes.' Rupert's voice was cold. 'To the South of France. I sought diversion at some length, and found it not, so I eventually gave up and came home to get on with the book. I had no success with that, either.'

Sarah looked at him cautiously. 'Why?'

He shrugged. 'I think writer's block is the popular term. I was stuck for an opening. The words were dammed up in my head, but they flatly refused to come out. I tried alcohol as a loosening agent, but, like the pleasures of the Cote d'Azur, it failed miserably.' His mouth curved in mocking self-derision. 'Any suggestions, Sarah?'

'Not really.' She looked round nervously for her

handbag. 'I'd better be on my way. Thank you for lunch.'

'Nonsense, Sarah. You provided the lunch. Without your timely appearance I would still be fathoms-deep in my alcoholic stupor.' His voice sharpened as he rose to his feet, blocking her way. 'Was the reference really why you came?'

Sarah backed away, her eyes sliding from his. 'Of course——'

His hand shot out and seized her wrist in a bruising grip. 'Look at me, Sarah,' he grated.

Sarah's head came up reluctantly, until her eyes met the urgency in his. Her teeth sank into her trembling lower lip as, with an abrupt, comprehensive clarity, a curtain of self-delusion was pulled aside in her mind and she faced the truth. The reference had merely been a flimsy excuse, camouflaging the real motive that had driven her to seek Rupert out. With her free hand she brushed the hair away from a forehead suddenly damp with perspiration.

'There was another reason,' she said quietly. 'I came because there was a favour I wanted from you.'

'A favour?' He frowned, then slackened his hold on her wrist. 'So ask me!'

'Will you marry me, Rupert,' she blurted out, 'please?'

Rupert stood stock still, staring at her blankly in complete silence. After what seemed like hours to Sarah his eyes narrowed as they examined her pale, strained face, and he said softly, 'Why, Sarah? I find it hard to believe you are consumed with a longing to share my bed, nor does it seem likely that you are dying of love for me either.'

Oh I don't know, thought Sarah wildly, the way I feel isn't exactly making me feel very well. She collected herself with determination.

'I'm in trouble, Rupert,' she said bluntly, but not bluntly enough, apparently, as Rupert merely stared at her in blank incomprehension.

'What sort of trouble, Sarah? Are you short of money?' She withdrew her hand from his and clasped it together tightly with the other. 'Perhaps my terminology is dated,' she said shortly. 'I'm fairly sure I'm in an interesting condition if you prefer. If you find pregnancy interesting.' She kept her eyes down, afraid to gauge Rupert's reaction. When he finally spoke she could have sworn his voice quivered with amusement as he put out a finger and raised her unwilling face to his.

'How sure?'

The unexpected look of concern on his face almost put paid to Sarah's precarious composure. She took a deep breath.

'If you mean have I had any tests, no. Other indications would seem fairly conclusive, though.' Sarah licked dry lips, her eyes sliding away from his. 'I shall, of course, naturally understand if you aren't prepared to marry me. I'm sure there are other options——' She winced as his hand shot out and crushed both of hers.

'Other options! What the hell do you mean by that, woman?' His face was thunderous, and Sarah cowered away from his instinctively, all her defences down.

'Some girls manage on their own, or even——' Sarah faltered and decided against saying more.

'God grant me patience!' Rupert threw back his head, eyes shut and teeth tightly clenched. He flung away towards the window and stood there, looking out into the garden with his back to Sarah. Sarah stared at his broad shoulders in mutinous silence, fiercely resenting his anger. *She* was the injured party, after all. The present situation was a direct result of Rupert's reprehensible behaviour, and if anyone was entitled to go off like a rocket it was Sarah Morgan, not Rupert Clare. He swung round and came back to her, standing over her purposefully.

'I am angry,' he said in measured tones, 'not because you're pregnant—I acknowledge full responsibility for that. I'm angry, Sarah, at your doubts that there could be any possible course of action but marriage—and to me, I may add.'

'Do you imagine it was easy for me to ask?' she said quietly.

Rupert's face softened. 'No, Sarah—you must have found it hard to pocket your pride.'

Her head lifted instantly, and she gave him a cold stare. 'Let us say I would have done anything in the world to spare my parents a bastard as a grandchild!'

His mouth set grimly. 'Even bringing yourself to marry me!'

She nodded coolly. 'Even that.'

They glared at each other with dislike, then abruptly Rupert relaxed. 'There seems little point in scrapping with each other, Sarah. Let's go and sit in the study while we make plans. It's too hot in here.'

Acknowledging the sense in his suggestion Sarah followed him meekly across the hall to the study, making no demur when he steered her away from her usual seat at the table to sit beside him on the chaise longue. Rupert turned towards her, suddenly reaching out a hand to smooth her hair away from her heavy eyes.

'What can I say, Sarah? I deeply regret that this has happened.'

Her eyes hardened at the word regret. 'No more than I do, Rupert, I assure you. Shotgun weddings aren't my idea of fun, particularly in my father's own church. If you mean to marry me I'm afraid that's where the ceremony will have to be.'

Rupert nodded. 'Do they know we no longer——'

'No,' interrupted Sarah quickly. 'My father's heart is in far worse condition than I thought. A disturbance with Mari-Sîan over a mere party was enough to threaten a heart attack—I quail at what my little piece of news might do to him.'

Rupert looked sincerely concerned. 'Is your father better now?'

'Yes. A visit from the newly-weds put him back on his feet again, happily.'

'How were they?'

Sarah smiled, a touch of wistfulness in her eyes. 'Happy as sandboys. Rhia is a different person. Charles Hadley isn't so much a husband as a catalyst! Rhia has no regrets for the life she's left—apparently all she wants is to be a good wife, a good stepmother to the girls, and to provide the latter with a couple of brothers or sisters.'

Rupert took Sarah's hands in his, holding them lightly in his strong, warm clasp as he looked at her soberly. 'Is that what *you* want, Sarah?'

Her smile faded. 'Hobson's choice, Rupert, or do I mean Catch 22? We appear to be prospective parents whether we like it or not.'

Immediately a blank expression replaced the tenderness in his eyes and he released her hands. 'Right. Down to brass tacks, then Sarah. You want the wedding at home, then?'

'No, I do not.' Sarah drew a long breath. 'The thought brings me out in a rash. But I don't see any way round it.'

Rupert leapt to his feet and began to pace around the room. 'No, I see that. I'm sorry—God, I seem to do nothing but apologise.' He shook his head, as if to clear his brain, wincing as the ache in his head made itself felt. 'All right then, quiet wedding as soon as possible. Any preference for a honeymoon?'

Sarah's eyes smarted for an instant. Rupert appeared to have forgotten the Greek Islands. 'I don't really see the need for one,' she said practically. 'You need your book finished and if morning sickness is to be part of life for a while travelling doesn't appeal.'

The look he gave her was hostile, but he refrained from comment and scribbled in his diary. 'Quiet wedding,' he muttered. 'No honeymoon. Instructions for the reception please?'

Sarah glanced at him suspiciously. 'I leave that to you,' she said coolly. 'Shall I give Mrs Dobson a ring and say you're slightly more human now?'

He grinned. 'Do you think she'll come back just like that?'

'She likes me. I'll tell her we're getting married. That ought to do the trick, unless someone more civilised has lured her away.'

Sarah was right. Mrs Dobson would be back the following day.

'I should give her a rise,' advised Sarah. 'The Mrs Dobsons of this world are hard to come by.'

'Can I afford it now I have added responsibilities?' His tone was teasing, but it flicked Sarah on the raw.

'Don't worry, Rupert.' She smiled at him with saccharine sweetness. 'I'll try not to cause you too much expense—you'll only have *one* child to provide for, I can assure you.'

'I see.' Rupert stood with his hands in his pockets, rocking back and fore on his heels. 'So now we know exactly where we stand.' His eyes hardened to green flint as his eyes met the defiance in Sarah's head on.

'But Rupert, you made it crystal clear in your note that I fall far short of what you want in a wife.'

'You were quite lucid on my own shortcomings as a husband, if my memory serves me correctly,' he riposted with heat.

They stared at each other, then Sarah shrugged and got up to sit in her usual seat behind the table.

'Then as neither of us is delirious with joy over our forthcoming union we must try to resign ourselves to it as best we can.'

His smile had a lupine quality as he sat on a corner of the table, swinging one long leg as he leaned towards her confidentially.

'There's always the loophole of divorce, little dragon!'

Sarah eyed him judiciously. 'Personally I object to divorce on principle—but I shan't rule out the possibility. There's a first time for everything.'

'How very true, Sarah!' The smile widened.

Sarah controlled herself with an effort, her face blank. 'In that case, of course, there would be custody to consider.'

The smile vanished from Rupert's face instantly. 'If I am marrying you because of the child——' he began angrily.

'I didn't presume there was any other reason!'

'The child is mine.'

'Ours!'

Green eyes glared into blue, all semblance of cordiality gone, leaving a white-hot current of hostility that leapt between them like a laser beam.

'The child would stay with me,' said Rupert, his face mask-like with fury.

'Try taking it from me,' challenged Sarah.

Abruptly Rupert relaxed and slid from the table. 'Then we'd better do our best to get used to living together, and, if humanly possible, liking it.'

'I suppose we had,' said Sarah unenthusiastically.

Rupert patted her shoulder impersonally. 'Don't be too unhappy, Sarah. We could do worse, both of us.'

She gave him a crooked little smile. 'And if I've panicked? A false alarm, I mean?'

He rubbed his jaw, frowning at her. 'Have you ever—I mean, dates and so on. . . .' To Sarah's surprise colour showed through the taut brown skin on his cheekbones.

'Clockwork. Even when I had the accident. And I've never had morning sickness before either.' She looked at him curiously. 'That's an odd expression on your face, Rupert.'

'Resignation, darling. Or what is that pretty endearment your father uses—cariad?'

'Endearments in any language seem rather inappropriate under the circumstances.' said Sarah with dignity, and turned to her typewriter. 'Now. If you'll leave me in peace I'll get on with these tapes or you'll be getting meaningful digs from your agent.'

'You mean you want to start work for me right now?' Rupert looked taken aback.

'And shall continue. Until our surprise package puts in an appearance, anyway.' Sarah was deliberately brisk as she removed the cover from the machine. 'Although I think it's high time you invested in a word-processor for me.'

'Anything you say.' He gave her a mocking little bow, then waved a hand at the telephone. 'Ring up your parents and tell them the news, and book the church for the first convenient date while you're at it.'

'What exactly do you mean by "news", Rupert?'

His eyes softened as the met hers. 'Tell them I refuse to wait a moment longer before tying the knot. Let's leave the rest as long as possible, in deference to your father's health. After we've been married some time it won't come as so much of a shock.'

Sarah nodded gratefully, and began to dial. 'Hello, Mother? Yes, I'm fine, how are you—and Dad? Good. Listen, Mam, I hope you haven't packed your wedding-hat away. . . .'

CHAPTER TEN

THE village of Cwmderwen had barely recovered from
Rhiannon Morgan's wedding before her father set it
humming again by publishing the banns of Sarah's
marriage to Rupert Clare. Some people had thought
Sarah was engaged to Rhodri Lloyd-Ellis, others believed
there had been confusion over names and it must have
been her author all along, but no one actually questioned
Mrs Morgan on the point and as a result there was plenty
of food for speculation in the small, close-knit community.
The Rector ignored it with serenity, as usual, and Mrs
Morgan was so excited and pleased about her daughter's
happiness that any would-be questioners were disarmed.
The only cloud in Elizabeth Morgan's sky was Sarah's
insistence that the wedding be very small and as quiet as
possible, giving her father's fragile health as her reason.

'I've no wish to put your parents to any more trouble
than necessary,' said Rupert, 'so we'll have the reception
at a hotel; whichever one you want.'

Sarah vetoed that idea at once. 'I'd prefer a very
simple affair at home. I'll organise a caterer to do the
food so that Mother is free to enjoy herself, but it will still
be just a family party.'

'Whatever you want. I'll foot the bill of course.'

'No—thank you. I'll manage that part myself,' she said
coolly, and picked up the next cassette, ready to resume
typing.

Rupert looked at her in exasperation. 'You enjoy
being perverse!'

'Not at all. As it's in *my* home I prefer to pay for the
reception.'

'Your home is here with me from now on,' he
reminded her.

'I'm trying to accustom myself to the idea,' she said,

and sat with hands poised over the typewriter keys. With a smouldering look at Sarah's withdrawn face Rupert turned on his heel and stalked out of the room, closing the door behind him with an exaggerated care that irritated her more than the anticipated bang.

Sarah threw herself into her work with a concentration that managed to shut out thoughts of the fast approaching wedding until she was back in her flat each night. Relations between Rupert and herself grew more strained with every passing day and she felt below par most of the time, particularly in the mornings. One of the main bones of contention between them was the fact that she refused point blank to move into Rupert's house before the wedding, neither would she allow him to fetch her in the mornings or take her home at night. To his fury she was equally stubborn about spending every weekend at the rectory on her own with her family, leaving him kicking his heels in impotent rage in London while she spent her time in preparation for the wedding.

Mari-Sîan's A-level results had been as brilliant as expected and there was an air of euphoria in the Morgan household that Sarah had no wish to spoil by revealing the real reason for the wedding. By pleading fatigue she had her breakfast brought to her in bed, and stayed there until midmorning while she was at home, and managed to conceal her queasiness very successfully. Rupert's absence was explained by his wish to get as much work done on the new book before their wedding as he could, which seemed to satisfy the family, to Sarah's relief. It would have been beyond her to keep up the charade of pre-nuptial bliss her family would naturally expect if she and Rupert were together.

A further cause for argument, not only from Rupert, but from her mother and Mari-Sîan, was the matter of Sarah's wedding dress. To Sarah it seemed wasteful and unnecessary to buy another expensive outfit when the one bought for Rhia's wedding was perfectly suitable, including the hat.

'But everyone will have seen it,' remonstrated Mrs Morgan in distress. 'Let us buy you something new——'

Sarah was adamant and refused firmly. When Rupert discovered she intended wearing the same dress his face darkened and took on the now familiar look of baffled fury.

'I'm well aware that your approach to our wedding is far short of enthusiastic, Sarah, but surely to God you can invest in a new dress, if only for the look of the thing. I'll pay for it if that's the stumbling block.'

'No it's not,' she snapped. 'Besides, you must learn that money can't buy you everything in life, Rupert. It isn't the answer to my particular problem.' She turned back to her keyboard, missing the oddly hopeless look that shadowed his face for a fleeting moment.

'You're right, of course,' he said flatly. 'Wear what you like.' This time he did shut the door with a bang, which gave Sarah a fleeting moment of satisfaction before she retreated into the dull apathy that held her in thrall most of the time.

One morning Sarah woke up to a cool wet day, and put on a slim wool skirt instead of a summer dress. To her dismay she had difficulty pulling up the zip and no success at all in doing up the buttoned waistband. Stricken, she viewed herself from all angles in the mirror, and though there was little visible difference in her appearance the fact remained, her skirt was tight. Feverishly she took the satin dress from its padded hanger and slid it over her head, pulling and patting the narrow garment over her hips and tried to fasten the zip. There was no point in deluding herself—there was no question of wearing *that* particular dress on her wedding-day or at any other time, until she had parted with the little intruder who was making such a hotch-potch of her life.

'You're late,' said Rupert when Sarah arrived much later, with a face like thunder. 'Are you feeling off-colour?'

'No more than usual,' she said pettishly and scowled at him. 'I'll need tomorrow off.'

His eyebrows rose. 'Any particular reason?'

'I'll have to buy a new dress. The other one doesn't f-fit me any more.' To her disgust Sarah began to cry. Tears spilled down her face and splashed her shirt, and she put her knuckles in her eyes like a miserable child. Without a word Rupert picked her up and sat on the chaise longue, holding her close and rocking her to and fro until her tears stopped and she sat up sniffing, very conscious that her eyelids were swollen and the end of her nose frankly red.

'Sorry.' She pulled away from him, taking a deep, sobbing breath. 'It was a bit of a surprise, that's all. I didn't expect—I mean, it's so *soon*!'

Rupert drew her back in his arms and stroked her hair gently. 'No one could possibly tell, Sarah, you look just as skinny as ever to me.'

'Thanks a lot!'

'I'll give you some money—no. No argument,' he said sternly. 'And tomorrow you stay in bed all morning, then go and buy the most stunning dress you can find, plus all the bits and pieces, and come back here afterwards and have dinner with me. I'll tell Mrs Dobson to leave us something special. What do you fancy?'

'Chilli con carne?' Sarah raised hopeful eyes to his grinning face.

'Is that entirely suitable under the circumstances?'

Sarah scrambled off his lap, suddenly self-conscious. 'Probably not, but I fancy it madly.'

'Then of course you must have it.' Rupert looked up at her with an indulgent expression in his eyes that made Sarah's tears well up again for some reason.

'Thank you, Rupert. I—I'll go and ask Mrs Dobson for some tea.' This time it was Sarah who beat a hasty retreat, Rupert's kindness affecting her deeply.

From then on their relationship improved slightly for the few days remaining before the ceremony, a state of armed truce existing between them that never managed to revert to the moments of intimacy when Sarah cried in Rupert's arms, but was a decided improvement on the barely concealed hostility of before.

They were married on one of those golden days of early October, a faultless backdrop for this controversial, unique day in Sarah's life. She and her father spent a quiet half hour together in the church during the morning for a few moments of personal and private communion, Glyn Morgan's handsome silvery head bent towards Sarah protectively as the two pairs of blue eyes looked deep into each other without reserve.

'Is everything well with you now, Sarah?' He touched a gentle fingertip to the little notch at the bridge of her nose, and she knew very well he was not referring to her health, nor to her wedding, but to her outlook on life. With truth Sarah was able to reassure him.

'Yes, Dad. I've come to terms with life at last. I know I've given you cause for worry in the past and I'm sorry.' She smiled at him ruefully. 'Every family has its black sheep, I suppose.'

Glyn Morgan bent and kissed his daughter's forehead. 'I beg to differ. There's never been one in ours, cariad.'

'Thank you, Dad.'

He shook his head, his eyes very serious. 'There is nothing to thank me for, Sarah—quite the opposite. I blame myself for not being more understanding, for almost driving you from home. You've heard me preach from the text often enough in this very pulpit; "perfect love hath perfect understanding". I, of all people, should have known better how to practice what I preach.'

Her father's words made Sarah so happy that Rupert Anthony Clare was confronted by a bride incandescent with joy. As she put her hand in his he was so patently bemused that everyone present smiled indulgently as the Rector joined him in marriage to Sarah Elizabeth Morgan, a vision of loveliness in a Gino Ferrari dress of floating ivory silk printed in china blue, white rosebuds cascading over the dipping brim of her blue straw hat.

The simple, moving ceremony was quickly over and the guests returned to the rectory, where the reception immediately developed into the type of gay, intimate party never achieved at bigger, more formal wedding breakfasts. The hired caterers circulated with delicious food and vintage champagne, the latter doing much to encourage the flow of witticisms flying fast and furious as some of Rupert's friends, mostly from publishing and the press, mingled with the Morgans and their guests and close relations. Mari-Sîan's vivacity almost rivalled that of the bride as she flitted from group to group in all the glory of a slinky dark red dress, the impetus for a burst of diligent dieting. Rupert's best man, his editor Tom Harvey, looked from Sarah to Mari-Sîan, then across the room to where Rhia and Charles stood chatting to Naomi Prentiss and her husband, Theo Levison. He whistled and shook his head.

'My God, old son, if genes have anything to do with it you and Sarah here should produce a string of world beaters in the shape of offspring.'

The flaring tide of colour in Sarah's face did her no discredit in the eyes of the assembled company, particularly as it deepened when Rupert's arm tightened round her waist in instinctive protection.

Rhia came drifting across to them, breathtaking herself in strawberry pink chiffon with a cluster of silk carnations in her hair instead of a hat. She gave a meaningful look in Naomi's direction. 'Darling, how civilised you are! I don't know that I could have been so generous if Charles had wanted to invite former lights of love to *our* wedding.'

'My idea, not Rupert's,' said Sarah quickly, her eyes sparkling. 'And now I've actually met her I'm very glad. She's so bubbling and unaffected. I like her.'

Rhia gave a sly glance at Rupert. 'I don't see Rhodri Lloyd-Ellis here. Wouldn't you let Sarah invite him, brother-in-law?'

Rupert raised a quizzical eyebrow. 'Sarah never raised the subject. Which is just as well—magnanimity was never my strongest point.'

Sarah gave him a seraphic smile. 'I do love a man who can acknowledge his own shortcomings,' she said sweetly, but her composure wobbled slightly as Rupert bent swiftly and kissed her smiling mouth.

'While I just love to hear you say you love me, my darling.' The intimacy of his voice was deliberate, and Rhia laughed, wagging a finger at him in mock disapproval as she moved back to join her husband and Gareth and Jane.

The party looked all set to continue for some time after all the toasts were drunk and the speeches made, but after a while Rupert and Sarah made their departure, parrying all the expected queries as to their destination. It was only when the Corniche was gliding away from the waving cluster of guests that Sarah was able to relax completely, and with a sigh she tossed her hat carelessly in the back and settled comfortably in her seat.

'Tired?' Rupert kept his eyes ahead as he made for the by-pass.

'Not exactly. I ate rather a lot and drank more champagne than is probably good for me, but I feel pleasantly mellow.' She stretched luxuriously. 'I wonder where they imagine we're going—Paris, Rome, Bognor——'

Rupert laughed shortly.

'Anywhere but St John's Wood, no doubt.'

'Will Mrs Dobson be there when we get back?'

'No,' he said curtly. 'She assumed, not unnaturally, that we want the place to ourselves for a day or two. She'll be back on Friday morning.'

'Oh.' Sarah flushed, and kept the conversation to events of the day as they left the by-pass at Newport to join the M4 for London. It was pleasant driving with the setting sun behind them, and shortly after dark they arrived in Hamilton Terrace, where Rupert left the car in the converted coach house before following Sarah into the house with their luggage.

The house was very quiet and still. Sarah smiled nervously at Rupert and caught sight of the note on the hall table addressed to 'Mrs Clare' in Mrs Dobson's handwriting.

'I'm not "Sarah" any more,' she said, making a face, and read that the housekeeper had left several cold dishes ready in the refrigerator, and various other delicacies were in the freezer for consumption until Mrs Dobson's return.

'I'll take the bags up,' said Rupert stiffly, and went up the curving staircase. Sarah trailed meekly after him, hat in hand, secretly rather dismayed by the attitude of her brand-new husband, whose bonhomie appeared to have been left behind at the reception.

'Which room is mine?' she asked.

Rupert entered his own bedroom and dumped the cases on the floor as Sarah hovered in the doorway. 'This one,' he said shortly.

Sarah stiffened. 'I know I said "anywhere" when you asked me last week where I wanted to sleep——'

'And I know that what you really meant was anywhere but here. Nevertheless I think it best you occupy the master bedroom, ostensibly with me.' He sauntered over to one of the mirror-fronted doors in the cupboards along one wall and opened it. To Sarah's surprise it led to a small dressing room. She took a quick look inside and saw a single bed made up in readiness.

Rupert moved along to another door and smiled coolly. 'The bathroom.'

'I remember.' Sarah was frowning. She had thought the room was imprinted on her memory for all time, but tonight it looked different. 'I only saw it for a moment,' she said slowly, 'but I had an impression of browns and golds.' Her eyes went from the white carpet to the white Spanish cotton spread on the bed, the great semicircular bay window curtained in aquamarine raw silk and the small love-seat upholstered in dove grey velvet, with cushions in white and coral.

'I had the room redecorated.' Rupert was hanging up his formal clothes in one of the cupboards. 'When you finally went off to Monmouth last week the decorators came in. I hope you like it.' He kept his back turned as he took out jeans and shirt.

Sarah was impressed by his thoughtfulness, at a loss for the right thing to say. 'It's perfect, Rupert. Thank you.'

She smiled diffidently. 'I like the Hockney; the other picture, too. Is that new?'

Rupert nodded as Sarah examined the splash of red poppies against a background of partly harvested corn, the colours raw and brilliant in the subtle coolness of the room.

'A wedding present, Sarah. I'm glad it meets with your approval.' He went through into the dressing room and shut the door, leaving Sarah standing in the middle of the room with no idea what she should do next. The past weeks had gone by in a frenzy of work and preparations for the wedding, giving them no opportunity to be awkward with each other. Now that they were finally alone together Sarah felt gauche and tongue-tied, nervous as a cat. When Rupert emerged in jeans and shirt to find her standing exactly where he left her he smiled, shaking his head impatiently.

'Come on, slowcoach. Why not get into something more comfortable? Dressing gown if you like, then come down to the drawing room. I'll have the mandatory champagne waiting and some music on the stereo, or you can watch television, if you like.'

Sarah laid her hat on the velvet seat. 'Yes. Fine. I'll be down shortly.'

She took off her dress and hung it in the section of wardrobe she found to be hers after investigation, then stood irresolute in her white silk slip before opening her case to find something to put on. She frowned at the extravagant apricot crêpe-de-chine confection Rhia had given her, and knew very well she could never summon up enough courage to float downstairs in that. After a swift shower she slid on one of the thin white cotton nightgowns she normally wore, covering it with a long robe of kingfisher velvet, her one personal gesture towards a trousseau. As she went downstairs the music rising to meet her was sombre, yet romantic, familiar even though she failed to put a name to it. The door to the drawing room stood open and she hovered silently in the doorway, feeling like an intruder in the formal, beautiful room she had seldom entered. The focal point of the room was the fireplace at the far end; itself a mere brass-bound aperture in a great square mirrored surround rising to the intricately carved cornice. She could see her reflection in the mirror, a surrealist impression of black and white and vivid blue. The music rose and swelled, the haunting melancholy of the solo oboe plucking at her heartstrings, shivering through her as she stood, riveted to the spot. Between the long white settees that faced each other across the middle of the room stood a brass-bound glass table with champagne in a silver bucket, flanked by champagne flutes and a silver tray, its contents veiled by a glossy starched napkin.

Rupert lay prone on one of the white settees, inert, relaxed, an arm over his eyes, unaware of Sarah's presence. She knew she should go in. The scene was set, the music playing, the curtain up, but she had no idea of her lines. She coughed delicately. 'Is it Sibelius?' she asked quietly.

Rupert's arm dropped and he rose, nodding. '"Swan of Tuonela." Well come on in. Don't just stand there.'

Sarah could detect no warmth in his eyes as she crossed the expanse of cinnamon carpet, its pile silky to the soles of her feet. He looked down at her toes.

'Should your feet be bare?'

'I never wear slippers.'

'Then come and put your feet up here and have something to eat.' He handed her a plate and offered her the silver dish, which held a variety of delicacies, smoked salmon sandwiches, lobster patties, small slices of quiche Lorraine. Sarah found she was hungry and ate with appetite, drinking the champagne thirstily as if it were lemonade. Rupert sat opposite, eating little, but refilling his glass with regularity, the handsome formal bridegroom transformed into a brooding male in a frankly ancient white shirt and faded jeans, with feet as bare as her own. The music was the only sound to break the silence as Sarah helped herself to another lobster patty, more for something to do than because she wanted it. When the music stopped Rupert got up and moved to the stereo.

'Could we have something a little, well, happier this time?' asked Sarah, who found Sibelius too poignant and moving under the present circumstances.

'We've never discussed music.' Rupert had his back to her going through a pile of records. 'I have no idea what you like—or even if you like music at all.'

'You dare ask me that when my name's Morgan!'

He swung round, his eyes glittering. 'Not any more. It's Clare now.'

Sarah smiled brightly. 'So it is. I must try to get used to it.'

'So what would you like? Brahms, Debussy, the Beatles, Delius?'

'I like opera best.' Sarah exaggerated her accent. 'Fond of the voice we are in Wales, you know.'

Rupert grinned, to her relief. 'I think Richard Strauss and "Der Rosenkavalier" is about as close as I can get.'

'Lovely.'

The music helped a little, but not much. While they finished off the champagne Sarah chattered about the wedding, even going so far as to say how much she'd liked Naomi.

'I feel she and I could be friends.' Sarah smiled uncertainly at Rupert.

'A pity you hadn't felt that way earlier. It would have saved a lot of trouble.' Rupert kept his eyes on his drink, his face shuttered and withdrawn.

Sarah tried another tack. 'I liked Tom Harvey too—I had quite an amusing chat with him. You were nobly attempting to converse with Aunt Clarice at the time. How did you manage?'

'Not very successfully. For one thing that hearing aid of hers appears to be defective, and the other drawback was mistaken identity. She seemed to be under the impression I was Rhodri Lloyd-Ellis.'

Sarah gave a nervous little giggle, then wished she hadn't as Rupert's eyebrows drew together ominously.

'I'm glad you find it amusing. I did not.'

After that the conversation died. By the time the lush,

evocative lilt of the Rosenkavalier Waltz filled the room Sarah had had enough. She drained the rest of the champagne in her glass and put it down on the tray, feeling tired and flat and disinclined to make any further effort.

'Just for tonight would you mind seeing to the plates and things?' She stifled a yawn against the back of her hand and stood up, weaving about a little to her embarrassment as she did her utmost to stand erect.

'You're stoned,' Rupert informed her laconically and took her arm.

Sarah shook his hand off crossly.

'I am not,' she said with dignity. 'I am merely a little tired. I was up early this morning, there was all the strain of the wedding ceremony, and we had a long drive after the reception.'

His face softened as he put out a hand to steady her. A smile lit in his eyes as they met hers. 'And you've just spent some time trying to make conversation with a morose swine who wouldn't join in. You are fully entitled to feel tired, Mrs Clare.'

'I also happen to be pregnant,' said Sarah, with a clarity she regretted instantly as the light snuffed out in his eyes like a doused candleflame.

'Do you imagine that for a single instant I ever forget?' he demanded roughly.

Sarah removed his hand and began what seemed like an endless journey towards the door. 'I'm going to bed, Rupert. Goodnight.'

With an exasperated sigh he followed her and picked her up. 'If you intend getting there tonight you'd better accept a lift.'

Sarah closed her eyes, her equilibrium infinitely worse as Rupert mounted the stairs with her, his breathing growing more laboured as he reached the top.

'You'd better put me down if I'm that heavy,' she said. 'I'd hate to give you a heart attack.'

With a look of dislike he entered the bedroom, rammed the light switch on with his elbow and dumped her unceremoniously on the bed, then bit his lip in annoyance. 'I apologise. I didn't mean to jar you.'

'Not at all,' answered Sarah politely. She rolled over and got to her feet on the other side of the bed.

'Where the hell are you off to now?'

She gave him a withering look and went unsteadily across the room. 'To the bathroom.'

When she got back the coral-shaded bedside lamps were the only light in the room, and the bed was neatly turned down. Rupert slid the robe from Sarah's shoulders without ceremony.

'Go on, get in,' he ordered.

Sarah flashed him a mutinous look, but did as he said, lying against the pillows looking small and defenceless, the shadows suddenly pronounced beneath her eyes. Rupert draped her robe over the grey velvet of the dressing-table stool and went to the door.

'I'm going downstairs to clear up the drawing room, then I'll come back and sleep through there. If you're asleep I'll try not to disturb you—is there anything you want?'

'Yes. I'd like a dog.'

Rupert stared at her dumbfounded.

'A dog? What made you think of that now?'

Sarah turned dreamy eyes on him and smiled. 'I was thinking of the garden. It's big. Plenty of room for a puppy, it would be company until the baby arrives. I'd like something of my own to cuddle.'

Rupert's face looked harsh in the shadows beyond the lamplight. 'Wouldn't we all, Sarah!'

His words floated in the air after he left, the irony in his voice remaining with Sarah as she fell asleep.

Before long she was back in the usual car, careering along the same narrow, twisting road in the dark, hurtling round bends, the headlights picking up eyes in the hedgerows, feral golden gleams as the tyres screeched on a road surface suddenly slick and greasy as heavy rain fell on asphalt dry and warm from a heatwave. Heavy drops spattered the windscreen, the wipers ineffective against the sudden onslaught as the car screamed round that final corner and, in the instant that she realised it would never make it the car shot off the road and someone was screaming far away as it plunged and something banged her head. She twisted and moaned, her arms clasped on the wheel and there were people and broken glass and pain, and someone calling her name.

'Sarah—Sarah—for God's sake wake up! Sarah!'

She opened her eyes, sobbing hysterically, to see Rupert's face, frantic by the light of the lamp as he tried to wake her. With a sigh of relief he gathered her up against him, her tears running hot down his bare chest as he stroked her damp hair and kissed the top of her head, murmuring soothing sounds of endearment while his nearness and warmth restored Sarah to sanity. Sarah became aware that her nightgown was plastered to her body with perspiration as her shuddering gradually subsided, her gasps slowing until she was breathing almost normally.

'I had a nightmare,' she said unnecessarily, her voice thick and indistinct.

Rupert's hold tightened. 'I rather gathered that. You were having it at full stereophonic blast, sweetheart.'

'Sorry.' Sarah sniffed vigorously. 'Haven't had it for ages. Must have been the lobster.'

'You've had it before?' He held her away from him, his eyes dark with concern.

Sarah nodded glumly. 'I used to get it regularly after the accident. It went away eventually. I thought I was over it altogether—it's a bit disappointing to get it again.'

Rupert whistled softly, stroking the hair away from her forehead. 'You're soaked, darling. Can you manage a bath while I change the bed?'

Sarah nodded, flushing as she looked down at herself, and Rupert got up to fetch her robe, wrapping it round her. He gave her a pat on the bottom and steered her towards the bathroom.

'Go on, get a move on.'

Sarah ran the water into the circular bath and found a

flagon of bath salts, sprinkling in a generous handful before letting herself into the scented water with a sigh of bliss, lying back as she listened to the comforting sound of Rupert moving about in the bedroom. After a while he knocked on the door.

'I'm going down to get a drink, Sarah. What can I get you?'

'Something cold and non-alcoholic, please. Definitely no champagne.'

He laughed. 'Right. Don't fall asleep in there. Time you were coming out.'

With a sigh Sarah heaved herself up and rubbed herself dry, looking at herself critically in the huge mirror on the opposite wall, grimacing at her swollen eyes. She rubbed at her hair, then brushed it vigorously with one of Rupert's tortoiseshell brushes from a wide onyx shelf that seemed to contain very few aids to a man's vanity.

'Hurry up in there,' bawled Rupert.

'I've finished. Can you rummage in my case for another nightgown, please?'

With resignation Sarah accepted the handful of apricot crêpe-de-chine and lace Rupert held discreetly round the door, and slid it over her head, liking the feel of it, but averting her eyes from her reflection as she wrapped herself in the velvet robe and went back into the bedroom, where Rupert had placed a well stocked tray on the dressing table. He handed her a tall glass clinking with ice.

'Ginger ale. Will that do?'

'Lovely.'

'Get into bed first.'

Sarah obeyed, ridding herself of her robe and getting into bed as quickly as she could while Rupert held her drink. When she was settled against the pillows he handed her the glass, watching with eyebrows raised as she drained the cold, dry liquid almost in one gulp.

'Hey. Steady on,' he grinned at her. 'Want another one?'

Sarah shook her head, noticing for the first time that he

had added a red silk dressing gown to the black pyjama trousers he had on earlier, and his hair was smooth as though it had been brushed.

'I've been a nuisance.' She held his eyes steadily. 'I'm sorry, Rupert.'

He strolled over to the tray with her glass. 'As I said before, Sarah, there's nothing to be sorry for.' He came to the edge of the bed and stood looking down at her gravely. 'Can you sleep now? Shall I put the light out?'

Panic filled Sarah at the mere thought. She knew very well it was illogical. The nightmare had never recurred in the same night, though that was probably because she had never allowed herself to go back to sleep again, and at the moment the prospect of being alone in the dark reduced her to a jelly of fear. She looked up at his watchful face in appeal, a beseeching look in her blue eyes.

'Could you—would you stay with me for a while? I know it's childish, but I find it hard to shake these things off.' She smiled uncertainly. 'I promise you I won't have another one for ages.'

He smiled at her with the brilliant, reckless smile that had been missing for some time from his brooding, handsome face. 'In that case I'd better make the most of it while I can.'

Sarah had assumed he would sit on the bed holding her hand for a while once the light was out, but Rupert thought differently. He stooped to switch off the lamp, then there was a rustle, the covers were turned back and he slid in beside her.

'Oh, but——'

'But nothing,' he said forcefully. 'Come here.'

Without further ado Sarah found herself closed in Rupert's arms, her head on his bare shoulder, and immediately her fears seemed groundless. She was conscious of only a wonderful sensation of security and warmth, and could feel her body relaxing, curving against his as though this was how she always slept.

'Better?' His breath stirred in her hair, his arms tightening around her as she moved instinctively closer.

'M'm,' she murmured.

'Right, then, beautiful dreamer, let's hear all about it.'

Sarah stiffened. 'Not much to tell. I just think it's all happening again, that's all.'

'Sarah.' His voice was gently persistent. 'I heard you screaming.'

'I know. I'm sorry—I do sometimes.'

'Do you know what you scream?'

She shook her head, puzzled. 'You were shouting "Rhia, no, stop", at the top of your voice.'

Sarah slumped against him. 'Oh, I see.'

'So come on. Give.'

Sarah gave in, suddenly eager to unburden herself.

'Rhia was driving, not me, that's all. We'd been to a party. I'd wanted to leave long before, but Rhia was having a wonderful time. She was already becoming well known as a model, and the men were swarming round her, and she felt like celebrating because she'd just landed a plum modelling job. It was a new perfume— Primavera—perhaps you remember the campaign. They wanted a new face to identify with it—one with an aura of purity and youth that came across on the television screen.'

Rupert drew a deep breath, and held her closer, and after a moment Sarah went on. 'Up to then I'd only driven the car a few yards in a layby with Rhia, unknown to my father, and had only just sent off for my provisional licence. I knew where the pedals were, and just about how to change gear and that was all. So Rhia had to drive home, even though she'd had something to drink. I'd only been on lemonade, and honestly she'd not had all that much to drink, but she was on a great big high on adulation and success mixed in with the alcohol, and she drove a bit too fast. Father's car was old and the brakes failed. I can hear her now, shouting at me, telling me to jump out. She couldn't control the car. Just before that last bend she screamed "Now, Sarah, now!" but my seat-belt jammed and I couldn't undo it in my panic. She jumped and I didn't. There was an almighty skid as the car left the road and went into a ditch, and crack, I was out, but not for long. I came to in the driving seat with the car all slewed over on one side and Rhia imploring me to forgive her and say I was driving so she couldn't be breathalised. Then there were people everywhere and an ambulance came and next thing I knew I was in hospital with a broken jaw and a face like Frankenstein's monster, not to mention sundry other little injuries. Rhia just had bruises—not on her face luckily—and a dislocated wrist.' Sarah gave a muffled little laugh. 'She dislocated it dragging me from one seat to the other.'

Rupert's voice was evil. 'You let her get away with it?'

'I refused to say anything to anybody. It was a bit difficult to talk anyway. When they let Rhia see me she nearly passed out in horror. She was wild with remorse, determined to tell everyone what had happened. I persuaded her not to. At the time my emotions seemed dulled. Nothing mattered. And Rhia had the chance of this big job—and they wanted a snowmaiden, all purity and elusive glamour, the unattainable ideal that all men long for. She'd have been out on her ear if the truth were known.'

'Bloody hell!' Rupert sounded savage.

'Wait. I honestly didn't care. It was I who persuaded Rhia to leave things as they were. Unfortunately neither of us foresaw how things would work out in the long term, that when someone makes a sacrifice for someone else, both parties eventually feel resentment. We made our pact and got stuck with it. Through my own decision I became a sort of outsider, but I couldn't do anything about it because I was the one who'd insisted on it. And there was Rhia, the star, burdened with this crushing obligation.' Sarah moved as Rupert stirred against her. 'I must be boring you out of your head.'

'Far from it! What I don't see is why Rhia doesn't clear it all up. She's out of the limelight now; or would it dull the lovelight in Sir Charles's doting eyes?'

'Don't be snide. Rhia, for the first time in her life, is very much in love. She was afraid to tell Charles before they were married, but on their honeymoon she couldn't keep quiet any longer. It made no difference whatever to Charles, despite your suspicions, and Rhia came back from Venice determined to tell Mother and Dad and give me a clean slate.'

Rupert gave an exasperated sigh. 'So what stopped her?'

'I did. And I shall always be glad I did. Rehashing all that old grief and misery would have been terrible for my parents, and my father would never have recovered from the shock of knowing the blame had been in the wrong place all this time.' Sarah twisted round in Rupert's hold, heaving herself up so that her face was nearer his. 'Besides, it was all irrelevant. Father finally gave me his forgiveness and trust without hearing the truth—just as you wanted me to do about the scene with Naomi, Rupert. Faith and trust was what we both wanted, and I'm ashamed to say I wasn't strong enough to give it to you as my father did to me. Anyway, I told Rhia to keep mum, and neither of us now have any hangups about the entire thing—no resentment, no bitterness, it's over. And now for heaven's sake can I go to sleep?' Sarah yawned suddenly and violently, feeling exhausted. Rupert chuckled and settled her more comfortably, cradling her protectively in his arms.

'Catharsis can be tiring, sweetheart.' His lips touched hers very gently. 'Go to sleep.'

'Don't leave me, Rupert,' muttered Sarah indistinctly, burrowing her face into his neck.

'No chance,' he assured her, and with gratitude she settled herself happily for sleep.

Sarah woke hazily to darkness. Some time during the night she must have turned away from Rupert, and now she lay with her back encompassed by the curve of his body, his arm close about her waist. She lay very still for fear of disturbing him, liking the sound of his deep, even breathing, and the warmth of it on the back of her neck. She stared into the darkness with a wry, unseen smile as she remembered that this was her wedding night—a by no means run-of-the-mill occasion, by any standards. Then something in the altered tempo of Rupert's breathing told her he was awake. He made no sound but his body tensed and the arm around her tightened involuntarily before he tried very gently to draw it away. Sarah grabbed his wrist and held his arm where it was.

'Don't go,' she whispered. There was silence, and she wondered if Rupert had heard her. As she felt him draw a deep breath she relaxed, wriggling closer to him. 'Sorry I woke you,' she said apologetically.

'So am I.' His breath seemed hotter against the nape of her neck as he spoke.

'Oh.' Sarah bit her lip.

Rupert sighed. 'I don't mean I yearn violently for sleep, but now I'm awake I think it best if I go back to the other room.'

'Of course.' Offended, Sarah moved away from him to the edge of the bed.

'Let me put it in words of one syllable then, Sarah,' he said patiently. 'Any normal male who wakes up in the night with a beautiful girl in his arms is likely to want to make love to her. You, my dear, are not just any attractive female, you are now my wife and I love you. As I have this inconvenient tendency to want to make love to you wherever we are, whatever time of day it is, what sort of chance do you think I have of staying sane under these circumstances?'

Sarah lay still, wondering if he could hear the sound of her quickened breathing, also her heartbeats, which suddenly seemed to have become deafening. She knew Rupert was waiting for her to say something, but her voice seemed imprisoned in her throat.

'Our first experience together was disastrous,' he went on quietly. 'My behaviour was inexcusable. I was jealous as hell, and angry. I wanted to punish as well as possess, and I don't blame you for being disgusted, even terrified. Now, of course, I'm afraid to come near you. You've been arctic towards me ever since, and I presume that without the disastrous consequences you'd never have let me see you again.'

Sarah turned over towards him.. 'My hostility wasn't because you made love to me—for want of a better description—nor even because of the baby.'

Rupert raised himself on one elbow, trying to see her face in the darkness. 'What else did I do wrong, for God's sake?'

Sarah gave a stifled little laugh. 'The way you took off without seeing me afterwards, with only that wretched note to tell me I wasn't the sort of wife you wanted.'

'Is that how you took it? My God, Sarah, what a pair of morons we are. I fled the field with the idea of leaving it clear for Lloyd-Ellis. I thought that was what you wanted!'

'You didn't exactly leave the field clear,' she pointed out, then began to laugh softly. 'You left a little obstacle behind you!'

'Sarah——' he groaned and turned on his stomach, his face buried in the pillow. 'Do you mind very badly?'

'Not now I'm a respectable married lady. The thought rather threw me at first, but now I quite fancy the idea. I told you I wanted something to cuddle.'

Rupert raised his head.

'Must you have a dog? Why lavish your affections on some undeserving animal when you have a perfectly good husband going to waste?'

'Perfectly good?' she asked with a chuckle.

'Perhaps "perfect" was a little optimistic.' He moved a little nearer. 'But I meant all those vows in church today, Sarah. I intend to be as good a husband as humanly possible.'

Sarah's laughter turned into something nearer tears and she threw herself into the arms opened to receive her, raising her face fervently to Rupert's kiss. For a long, long interval they lay close, their arms locked about each other as he kissed her deeply, with all the hungry intensity dammed up inside him over the previous few weeks, Sarah's uninhibited response shaking him to the core.

When at long last he raised his head a little, Sarah

asked breathlessly, 'You haven't told me how *you* feel about approaching fatherhood.'

He held her closer his mouth against her neck. 'Frankly jubilant, especially if it should happen to be a little girl with eyes like yours.'

Sarah pulled away. 'It won't be if I can help it,' she said tartly. 'I intend to have sons. From now on I'm the only woman in your life, Rupert Clare.'

'That works both ways, madam,' he said swiftly, and gave her a little shake. 'No more amorous Welshmen for you either, or men of any other nationality if it comes to that.'

They laughed together, holding each other close. Rupert smoothed Sarah's hair away from her forehead with a slightly unsteady hand.

'What I said still applies, sweetheart. If I stay here I'll want to make love to you.'

'I should hope so. It's our wedding night, after all!' Sarah curved herself closer to him, taking a wicked delight in the violent tremor that ran through his long body.

'No hang-ups from last time?' he asked huskily.

'Not really. I'm depending on you to wipe the memory of that night out completely.'

'And if I don't?'

'You'll just have to keep trying until you do!'

Her laughter was stifled by his descending mouth, which caressed and played with hers endlessly before moving down her chin and along her jawbone in a series of featherlight kisses until he reached her ear, where he ran the tip of his tongue over the intricate whorls inside. Sarah's eyes widened in the darkness, startled at the delicate sensuality of the caress.

'That's more like it,' she said breathlessly.

Rupert stopped dead. 'More like what?' he enquired acidly.

Sarah snuggled against him. 'My first encounter with love—or sex—at your hands Rupert, displayed a glaring lack of finesse on your part. Frankly I was not only incensed but astonished.'

'You don't say?' he drawled, and drew away. 'No doubt you'll enlighten me why?'

'Certainly. I, if you remember, Rupert, used to fend off all those love-crazed females battering down your door, and I couldn't help feeling that your technique with them must surely have been a lot different.'

Rupert stirred restlessly. 'So?'

'I came to the conclusion a hundred other women couldn't be wrong—and perhaps I should give you a second chance!' For a moment Sarah thought she'd gone too far, alienating him yet again, then he pulled her hard against him and kissed her with anger and laughter mixed with a passion it was plain he no longer intended to keep in check.

'How very charitable, my analytical darling,' he growled, between kisses that made Sarah's head reel. 'Perhaps if I do well enough, you might even consider giving me a third, or even a fourth chance as well!'

It was broad daylight when Sarah raised heavy eyelids again, the sun filtering through the aquamarine curtains with a soothing underwater effect. Drowsily she turned to find Rupert lying on one elbow watching her wake. He smiled lazily and put out a fingertip to touch her bottom lip. Sarah kissed it gently and smiled at him, her eyes gleaming like jewels beneath sleepy half-closed lids. She yawned and stretched, turning her face up to his.

'Good morning. Kiss me awake.'

Rupert smiled and bent his head to oblige with an enthusiasm that made Sarah stretch like a cat beneath the sheet that covered them. She gave a blissful sigh as he raised his head.

'Just for the record, sleepyhead, it's good afternoon,' he informed her lazily.

Sarah felt guilty. 'Have you been awake long? I suppose we should get up.'

Rupert drew her to him. 'Why? I agree with Marlowe—"Jove send me more such afternoons as these!"'

They lay in silence for a long, dreamy interval, content to enjoy each other's nearness and the faintly illicit pleasure of being in bed on a sunlight afternoon.

'As a matter of interest,' said Rupert after a while, 'did I merit my second chance? You may remember that it was you who instructed me, at one interesting point, to be less gentle. Did I manage to achieve a happy medium?'

Sarah coloured, her eyes kindling at the recollection, then turned laughing, to look at his smug profile. 'Happy, yes. Medium had nothing to do with it.'

He leaned over and kissed her swiftly, then stretched away from her to open the drawer of his bedside table. 'Such a heartfelt, reassuring compliment deserves a reward.' He sat up to dangle a slender gold chain in front of her nose, swinging the small jade dragon pendant back and forth. Sarah looked at it in silence, biting her lip, then pushed herself up so that Rupert could fasten the chain round her neck. She looked down at the little dragon, turning it over in her fingers lovingly.

'It's exquisite, Rupert.' She reached up to kiss him. 'Also very appropriate—thank you.'

'Not quite as apt as I would have wished. Chinese instead of Welsh, but of impeccable ancestry I was assured.' Rupert looked down into her face questioningly. 'What is it? Don't you like him?'

'I adore him!' Sarah turned troubled blue eyes up to his. 'But I never thought—I mean, I have nothing for you, Rupert.'

He pulled her against him. 'That's where you're quite wrong, Sarah. I have the only gift I'll ever want, right here in my arms.'

Sarah's mouth trembled and she buried her face against his neck, muttering indistinctly against his skin.

'What did you say?' he demanded, laughing and nudging her face away.

'I said I now realise what it was those other women all found so irresistible. It's your way with words.'

Rupert grinned down into her eyes.

'Wrong again,' he teased. 'I think the general

consensus of opinion leaned more to action. Which is your preference?'

Sarah smiled back at him with a new, radiant assurance that had come into being overnight.

'It's *my* considered opinion that, speaking as your wife, Rupert Clare, I'm entitled to the lot!'

Share the joys and sorrows
of real-life love with
Harlequin American Romance! ™

GET THIS BOOK
FREE as your introduction to
Harlequin American Romance —
an exciting series of romance
novels written especially for
the American woman of today.

Mail to:
Harlequin Reader Service

In the U.S.
2504 West Southern Ave.
Tempe, AZ 85282

In Canada
P.O. Box 2800, Postal Station A
5170 Yonge St., Willowdale, Ont. M2N 6J3

YES! I want to be one of the first to discover
Harlequin American Romance. Send me FREE and without
obligation *Twice in a Lifetime.* If you do not hear from me after I
have examined my FREE book, please send me the 4 new
Harlequin American Romances each month as soon as they
come off the presses. I understand that I will be billed only $2.25
for each book (total $9.00). There are no shipping or handling
charges. There is no minimum number of books that I have to
purchase. In fact, I may cancel this arrangement at any time.
Twice in a Lifetime is mine to keep as a FREE gift, even if I do not
buy any additional books.   154 BPA BPGE

Name _____ (please print) _____

Address _____ Apt. no. _____

City _____ State/Prov. _____ Zip/Postal Code _____

Signature (If under 18, parent or guardian must sign.) _____

This offer is limited to one order per household and not valid to current Harlequin
American Romance subscribers. We reserve the right to exercise discretion in
granting membership. If price changes are necessary, you will be notified.

AMR-SUB-1R